THE CASE OF THE
Mystery
Mark

THE
NICKI
HOLLAND
MYSTERIES
1

ANGELA ELWELL HUNT

Here's Life Publishers

First Printing, May 1991

Published by
HERE'S LIFE PUBLISHERS, INC.
P. O. Box 1576
San Bernardino, CA 92402

Cover illustration and interior artwork by Doron Ben-Ami
Cover design by David Marty Design

Library of Congress Cataloging-in-Publication Data
Hunt, Angela Elwell, 1957-
    The case of the mystery mark / Angela Elwell Hunt.
        p.   cm.
    Summary: Nicki is determined to solve the mystery at Pine Grove Middle School
when a student's research paper is stolen and circumstantial evidence points to her new
friend Kim, a Korean American.
    ISBN 0-89840-306-5
    [1. Schools—Fiction. 2. Korean Americans—Fiction. 3. Prejudices—Fiction
4. Mystery and detective stories.] I. Title.
PZ7.H9115Cas   1991
[Fic]—dc20   91-13508
                           CIP
                           AC

To Deborah Wade Huff,
"a friend who loves at all times"

Laura　　**Kim**　　**Nicki**

Christine **Meredith**

Nicki Holland was riding to school with Laura Cushman in a chauffeur-driven Rolls Royce. As she leaned back into the leather upholstery she thought her seventh grade year was certainly starting out right. With a new haircut, new clothes, and a new friend, nothing could go wrong. Absolutely nothing.

Last year she had walked to school every day with her best friends Christine Kelshaw and Meredith Dixon, but since meeting Laura two months ago, Nicki's life had been spent in part-time luxury. At least when she was with Laura, that is. When she was at home, life was pretty much ho-hum normal.

Nicki could see Christine and Meredith up ahead, walking together. "Hey, Laura, can't we stop and pick them up? They'd love it!"

Laura looked a little doubtful, but she tapped on the glass that separated the driver from his passengers and pointed to the curb. He smoothly pulled over until the sleek car was alongside the startled girls.

"Hey, Christine! Meredith!" Nicki called, lowering her window. "Want to ride to school in style?"

Meredith dropped her jaw. "Is that you, Nicki?" she asked.

Christine giggled, but she only hesitated a minute. "Sure, we'll ride." They piled in and the car pulled out into traffic. "We wondered where you'd been all summer," Christine said to Nicki.

"I'm sorry I haven't been around much," Nicki answered. "But after I met Laura we spent a week on the beach, and then a week at Walt Disney World with her mother. Last week we were so busy shopping for back-to-school clothes I didn't have a chance to call either of you."

"That's okay, Nicki, we forgive you," Meredith sniffed, pretending to be mad. She wound a curl of her long, dark hair around her finger and smiled at Laura. "Even though our best friend has ignored us since you came along, it's nice to meet you. I'm Meredith Dixon . . . "

" . . . the brain," giggled Christine. "And I'm Christine Kelshaw of the famous Kelshaw clan."

"She means she has five brothers and sisters," Nicki explained to Laura. "And they're all redheads like Christine. If you ever want peace and quiet, *don't* go to Christine's house."

"Is this your car?" asked Meredith, her eyes bugging.

"It's my mother's," Laura smiled, a little uncomfortably.

Meredith and Christine looked at Nicki. "You've moved up in the world, huh, kiddo?" cracked Christine.

"Laura and I met at the mall," Nicki explained. "She was new and didn't know where anything was, so I helped her find Burdines." Nicki rolled her eyes. "You haven't gone shopping until you've gone shopping with Laura."

"I can imagine," murmured Meredith. "What are you, a model?"

Laura blushed and shook her head.

"She could be," Nicki said, sensing Laura's embarrassment. Laura was beautiful, even at twelve, and Nicki couldn't help feeling awkward around her. But she felt sorry for Laura just the same. She seemed so alone.

"Why don't you go to Beachcrest Prep?" Christine asked, as usual with more bluntness than tact. "That's where most of the other rich kids go."

"I wanted to go where Nicki went," answered Laura a little stiffly. "Nicki is my only friend in Pine Grove."

"Oh," murmured Christine.

"That's some accent," said Meredith. "Where are you from?"

"Georgia," Laura replied, blushing. Nicki loved Laura's southern accent. It gave her, well, class. Everything sounded dignified when Laura said it. *Ah'd like shrimp, puh-leese. Ah like the peach color bet-tuh.* But now Laura was quieter than Nicki had ever seen her.

The girls settled back and rode in silence. Nicki felt uneasy for Laura—being new was hard enough, being mega-rich would make things harder. Nicki knew the car alone was enough to drop jaws all over the campus of Pine Grove Middle School. Laura was going to need help, but Meredith and Christine were Nicki's best friends and she didn't want to sacrifice them to help Laura feel secure.

"You guys, I just know this is going to be a great year," Nicki ventured. "Together we four are going to be the best of friends! We'll be in home room together, take classes together, and no one will be able to tear us apart! Okay?"

Christine flashed a freckled grin and Meredith nodded, but Laura's eyebrows rushed together in worry. "Are you sure?"

"If Nicki says you're okay, then you're okay with us,"

Christine said, cheerfully snapping her gum. "But I really think you should tell your mother to forget the limo."

Laura was puzzled. "Then how will I get to school? I live out in Gatscomb Hills and it's too far to walk. Mother would die before she'd let me ride a bus."

"That's what you get for living out in the Hills," said Christine. "Most of the kids in school live either in our subdivision or in Levitt Park Apartments."

"I have an idea," said Nicki, her shoulder-length brown hair bobbing beautifully just as Laura's hair stylist had said it would. "Just have the driver drop you off at my house. Then we can all walk to school together."

"What if it rains?"

Christine laughed. "Then tell your mom to have you delivered in something a little more modest. A Rolls Royce won't do anything to help you fit in around here."

"More modest—like a Mercedes?"

Christine sighed. "Like a Ford."

Nicki, Meredith and Christine had Mrs. Balian for English in sixth grade, so Nicki was pleasantly surprised that Mrs. Balian was in charge of their seventh-grade homeroom. It was nice to walk into school on the first day of a new year and have a teacher who knew your name already.

There was a rumor floating around school that Mrs. Balian had once been a first runner-up in the Miss America Pageant, but no one had the nerve to ask her outright if it was true. How would you ask such a question? If you acted like you thought it was true and it wasn't, she'd think you were stupid for believing such a wild tale. If you acted like you thought it wasn't true and it was, she'd be insulted that you didn't think she was Miss America material. So no one asked and no one knew for sure. Nicki figured that's why rumors stayed rumors instead of becoming proven fact.

Mrs. Balian didn't care where anyone sat in homeroom. Meredith, Laura, Christine and Nicki sat in chairs in the far right corner of the room opposite the door so they could see everyone entering. After a long summer, it was good to see who was back and who had changed.

Scott Spence, tall and good-looking, was back and much improved over last year's sixth-grade edition. "I think he's grown six inches in three months," Christine giggled.

"I'd say five and three-quarter inches," deduced Meredith expertly, peering at him through her clear slide rule.

Nicki perked up. Last year she had the unfortunate distinction of being the tallest girl in the sixth grade, and she was always glad to see a guy who was growing. "You might be the same height as Princess Diana," her mother always told her, "and she's as graceful as a swan." But Nicki felt more like a flagpole with big feet. She imagined Princess Diana felt the same way, only she was a princess and couldn't show it.

Michelle Vander Hagen came in, conscious as always that she wore the unofficial label of Most Beautiful Girl in the school. She smiled at Mrs. Balian, flashed a dimple at Scott Spence, and waited until the quiet beauty of her presence hushed the noise around her before she chose a seat.

"There she is," Christine sighed. "Our sure bet for seventh-grade Fall Festival queen. It's too bad sixth graders can't elect a representative. She'd have a crown in her closet already."

"I don't know if I could stomach having Queen Michelle around for three years," Nicki grumbled. "It's going to be bad enough having her win this year and next."

"She'll probably be on the homecoming court every year in high school, too," Meredith said. "So you'd better get used to being in class with royalty."

"Michelle can be a royal pain," mumbled Christine. "She won't play hard in gym, she won't walk outside in the rain, and remember last year when we all went door-to-door selling candy bars? Michelle wouldn't help. She thought she might mess up her hair."

"You're just mad because she was on your relay team and you guys came in last place," laughed Nicki.

Christine folded her arms and pouted. "Thirty-two times!" she muttered. "The girl tried to put a basketball into the hoop thirty-two times and *still* didn't get it in! What's the good in being pretty if you're totally useless?"

Corrin Burns bounced into the room next, obviously as stuck on herself as she was last year. She practically pranced to the front of the room, smiling and sashaying to show off her new outfit. If Corrin wore a label at all, it was Miss Flirt of Pine Grove Middle School.

"She might as well say, 'Look at me! Look at me!'" muttered Meredith. "Doesn't she know well-mannered people don't *flaunt* themselves that way?"

"Corrin doesn't know much about well-mannered people," Christine answered. "She only knows about boys."

Julie Anderson and Heather Linton now surrounded Corrin, cooing and gushing over her hair, her nails and her clothes like the loyal sidekicks they were. Meredith turned her head away. "I think I'm going to be sick."

Nicki remembered that Meredith had an unpleasant experience with Corrin last year. Just because Meredith is black, Corrin seemed to think Meredith deserved whatever Corrin chose to dish out. Last year Corrin made the mistake of calling Meredith the "n-word" in gym, and sweet, brainy Meredith came within two inches of punching Corrin out.

The late bell rang finally, and Mrs. Balian stood up with her computerized attendance roster. She gave friendly smiles to each of the returning students, but her eyes shone with frank curiosity when she called, "Cushman, Laura." Everyone else was curious and peered at Laura too, and Nicki felt uncomfortable for her new friend.

But Laura was as comfortable in the sea of seventh-grade faces as she had been when she ordered *in French* at the restaurant where she and Nicki went after shopping one day. She faced everyone with a disarming smile, shifted her perfect posture slightly, and said, "Here, ma'am."

"It's nice to meet you, Laura," smiled Mrs. Balian. "Where were you before you moved to Pine Grove?"

"Atlanta, Georgia, ma'am. My mother and I moved here this summer after my father died."

"I'm very sorry," Mrs. Balian hadn't counted on hearing bad news. "But we're very glad to have you in school with us."

As Mrs. Balian continued to call the list of names, Nicki couldn't help but notice that a tiny frown now occupied Michelle Vander Hagen's perfect face. Could she possibly consider Laura a contender for the title of Most Beautiful? Michelle had held that unspoken position since fifth grade, but who knew what would happen this year?

Then Nicki overheard the thin voice of Corrin Burns: "A Rolls Royce? You're kidding!"

Oh, brother. Laura had better look out. Michelle might be disturbed by the competition Laura presented, but Perfectly Beautiful People rarely acted ugly. Corrin Burns, however, didn't know how to be silent or tactful.

Neither Michelle nor Corrin could possibly like the idea of a new girl that was pretty, sophisticated *and* rich, Nicki realized. Whatever this upcoming year held, there were bound to be fireworks.

2

M r. Padgett, the principal, was halfway through his morning announcements over the intercom when in walked another new student. The girl wore a dark skirt, a white blouse and black shoes—all unusual for a casual seaside Florida town like Pine Grove. But when she lifted her head to hand Mrs. Balian her registration form, the girls noticed she was Oriental.

"Japanese?" Nicki asked Meredith.

"No, silly, Chinese," whispered Christine.

"Welcome to Pine Grove Middle School and our class," said Mrs. Balian, smiling. "Students, this is Kim Park and this is her first week in America."

"She's from Korea," Meredith said simply. "Park is an old and honorable Korean name."

"How does she know these things?" Laura whispered to Nicki.

"Meredith knows almost everything," Nicki explained. "She reads encyclopedias for fun. Plus, her parents are both professors and what she doesn't know, she can usually find out."

Mrs. Balian looked up from the note that Kim had given her. "Kim and her family are here because her mother is on a waiting list for a kidney transplant," she told the class. "Since Kim speaks very little English, let's do everything we can to help her out, okay?"

The bell rang and everyone filed out to go to first period classes. Nicki and her friends had all chosen life science for first period, so they headed toward the biology lab.

In the hall the girls passed Corrin Burns, who had backed Kim Park into the wall. Corrin's sharp voice passed through the muffle of the crowd easily: "I think it's just great that a Japanese girl is here. You Chinks are good in math, right? You'll do my math homework for me, right?" Corrin slowly rocked back on her heels and smiled at Kim. "If you don't help me out, I can get you into real trouble with the American government. Do you understand?"

Kim had bowed her head when Corrin began, but now she raised it and looked away from Corrin. "I . . . no . . . speak . . . " she mumbled, her tear-filled eyes searching for help.

Meredith wasn't going to stand by and watch. "Corrin Burns, you leave her alone," she snapped. "Give the girl a break and do your own lousy math homework, if you can."

Corrin flushed red and opened her mouth. *Uh oh,* Nicki thought. *Everybody brace for something really mean.*

But Meredith was glaring at Corrin. "Don't say anything. Don't even think anything," Meredith said evenly, her dark eyes flashing. "You'll be much better off."

Corrin snapped her jaw shut and flaunted off down the hall. Christine and Laura stopped to comfort Kim. "It's okay," Laura smiled. "I'm new here too and we're both going to do just fine. Don't worry about any little ol' thing."

Kim looked at the four girls, then spoke. "I can get you into real trouble with the American government!" Out of Kim's mouth came Corrin's exact words in Corrin's thin, little voice!

"Did I hear that right?" Nicki asked Meredith.

"That's incredible!" shrieked Christine, and Meredith leaned in for a closer look.

Kim now smiled at Laura. "It's okay," she said in Laura's own honeyed tones. "Don't worry about any little ol' thing."

The four girls looked at each other in amazement, then collapsed into giggles while Kim smiled and pointed at her registration card. "First period, life science," she said in the unmistakable accent of the school's guidance counselor.

The girls stopped laughing and looked at her. "You're really something, Kim," Nicki said, "and we'll go with you to your science class. We're all in it together. But about these voices . . . "

"It's her gift," said Laura.

"It's amazing," said Christine.

"It's a scientific improbability," said Meredith.

"Whatever," Nicki went on, "I think you'd better concentrate on learning the language and keeping the voices to yourself for a while. Some people just wouldn't understand."

Meredith had Kim's ability analyzed by the time the first week of school had ended. "It's mimicry," she explained as the four girls walked to school. "Some birds, parrots for instance, are able to mimic human voices or sing the songs of other birds."

"But Kim isn't a bird," Nicki pointed out.

Meredith went on. "Some people are just good

mimics. I have to admit Kim's *really* good. I asked my dad and he said that since some people are born with the innate ability to recall the notes of musical pieces . . . "

"Like Nicki's perfect pitch?" Christine interrupted.

"Sort of. Nicki, you can hear notes or tones and immediately know what they are, can't you?"

Nicki nodded. She had been able to tell a G chord from a D chord and everything else in between for as long as she could remember.

"Well, there are people who can hear a musical piece and not only know what the notes are, but can recall them indefinitely. They could hear a piano piece and actually play it, perfectly, years later. Perhaps Kim was born with the ability to recall the pitches of people's voices."

Meredith paused to brush a stray curl out of her eyes. She looked dreamily off into the distance. "I'd love to use her as my science project. I'm going to call it 'Dixon's Hypothesis of Total Vocal Recall.' "

"What if she doesn't want to be a science project?" asked Christine. "My little brother Stephen tried an experiment on my little brother Casey, and both of them just got into trouble."

"What did they do?" Nicki asked.

"Stephen put peas in Casey's ears to see if they'd sprout. Mom had to take Casey to the doctor to have them taken out, and she made Stephen eat three helpings of peas at dinner for a week." Christine grinned. "We haven't had any experiments at our house in a while."

"I'll make it worth Kim's while," said Meredith. "I'll teach her English while I'm studying my hypothesis. She won't mind."

"What good are all those voices?" Laura kicked a pebble in the sidewalk. "I think it's really kind of spooky."

"Are you kidding?" Christine crowed, jumping ahead of the others and walking backwards. "You could be the life of any party! You could imitate people for hours!"

"I don't think Kim's the life-of-the-party type," Nicki reminded them. "She seems very quiet. She hasn't done anything to make any friends."

"She hasn't done anything to make enemies either," Meredith pointed out. "She isn't rude or hateful, and she doesn't make fun of people even though she could. She's probably just trying to learn English."

"Sure, just because she can mimic people doesn't mean she knows the language," Laura added.

"My piano teacher is always fussing at me for using my perfect pitch instead of reading all the notes," Nicki explained. "Maybe it's too easy for Kim to use her ability without learning what the words mean. We're going to have to help her learn to talk as herself, not everyone else."

"I'd really like to help," said Christine. "Imagine, the girl is in a strange country with a sick mother, surrounded by strange people."

"Mean people, too," added Meredith, remembering Corrin.

"Mean people, too. I'd love to show her that all Americans aren't like Corrin Burns."

"Why not?" Nicki nodded. "Everyone willing to help Kim learn to speak English, raise your right hand."

Four right hands went up together. It was decided.

Mr. Cardoza, the seventh-grade English teacher, walked to the chalkboard and wrote "Research Paper" in bold letters. In his level voice, Mr. Cardoza explained: "One-half of your grade this grading period will be a research paper. You are to choose any author, living or dead, and write a paper describing his life, his work and his writing style. You must also read at least one book by this author and include a report on that book. It's almost like two papers in one, so I suggest you get busy. Your papers are due in three weeks." He paused and looked over the class. "Neatness counts. Any questions?"

There were no questions, only groans. But Meredith raised her hand. "Mr. Cardoza, I'd like to do my paper on William Shakespeare."

"That would be fine, Miss Dixon, but wouldn't you rather report on a less prodigious author?"

Some kids snickered at his choice of words, but Nicki knew Meredith and Mr. Cardoza were on the same wave length. "I think that to do anyone less prodigious than Shakespeare would be a waste of effort," Meredith said, looking down her nose slightly at Mr. Cardoza. "Unless you'd like me to study Chaucer."

Nicki grinned at Christine. They knew Meredith's father had written *The Compleat Chaucer*, a thick book that was his chief claim to fame. Meredith knew what she liked, and thanks to her parents, she liked Chaucer and Shakespeare. She'd rather die than do a report on someone too easy, someone *alive*.

"You may do Shakespeare only if you do a thorough and complete job as I specified," Mr. Cardoza told Meredith. "That means you'll have to read one of Shakespeare's plays, and there are college students who aren't up to that."

"I can do it," Meredith said, nervously bouncing the

end of her pencil against her desk and consulting her mental calendar. "If you'll give me two extra days for the report."

Mr. Cardoza thought a moment, then smiled. "For such a project, two extra days is fine with me. Everyone else will hand in their papers on Wednesday, and I'll expect yours on Friday." He looked up as the bell rang. "If there are no further questions, class is dismissed."

3

Three weeks later, after hours of reading and research, Mr. Cardoza's seventh-grade English class assembled with their papers. Because she had spent the summer reading all 1,054 pages of *Gone With the Wind*, Nicki had done hers on Margaret Mitchell. Her father's secretary at the insurance office had typed it for her.

Mrs. Cushman had a private secretary type Laura's report on *Jane Eyre* and Charlotte Brontë. Laura carried the book and an embroidered handkerchief everywhere for three weeks. "It's just so beautifully *tragic*," she told the other girls, shaking her blonde hair out of her blue-green eyes. "Don't you just *love* to read a book that makes you cry?" She sighed. "I will not have lived unless I have a romance like Jane Eyre's."

Christine's report was handwritten. "I was lucky to get it done at all," she said, dropping into her seat.

"What book did you read?" asked Nicki.

Christine pulled a book from her backpack and tossed it in Nicki's direction.

"*Cockatiels*?" asked Nicki, laughing. "You read a book on cockatiels?"

"Yes," Christine sniffed. "Mr. Cardoza didn't say it had to be a *famous* book, for heaven's sake. I just grabbed the first book I could find at home. Mother's breeding cockatiels now, so that's what I grabbed."

"How did you find any information about the author?" Meredith read the book's cover. "Who is Howard S. Smythe?"

"I wrote the publisher and Mr. Smythe wrote back to me," Christine explained, raising her chin and glaring indignantly at Meredith. "I found out everything I needed to know, thank you."

Kim Park entered with her head down, as usual, and Nicki wondered how she kept from running into things. She quietly sat down in the first seat two rows over. "Hey, Kim," Meredith called. "Did you get your paper done?"

Kim looked up and shyly nodded. "I read *Bridge to Terabithia* by Katherine Paterson," she answered.

"Was it a good book?" Christine asked.

"Yes," Kim looked away modestly and nodded. "It was a good book about a boy and his new friend."

His new friend. The words echoed in an awkward pause and Nicki felt a little guilty. They had been so busy the past three weeks on their papers, they hadn't given much thought to their plan of helping Kim with her English. But she was bright and had improved a lot. Maybe she wouldn't really need their help after all.

The bell rang and the shuffling of feet gradually stopped. While Mr. Cardoza silently checked seats against his attendance chart, practically every girl in the room made her own unconscious check—Scott Spence was present and well. It was a nice feeling to know the most wonderful guy in school sat only a few rows away.

Nicki noticed that Kim was absently doodling on her notebook cover. Instead of the stupid messages or circles most people drew, Kim doodled in little pictures that Nicki figured were part of the Korean language. It was beautiful, artsy doodling, and Nicki wondered what the letters meant.

Suddenly Corrin Burns burst into the room. "Mr. Cardoza, someone has stolen my research paper," she blurted out. "Someone stole it from my locker and left this in its place!"

She held up a yellow sheet of paper. But it wasn't the color of the paper that was unusual—it was a mark in the lower right-hand corner: a lovely, delicate pair of Oriental figures.

Mr. Cardoza replied smoothly, "Miss Burns, you are late, you are loud and you've interrupted."

Corrin tossed her head. "I was going to be on time, but I stopped by my locker to pick up my research paper. I worked *so hard* on it, Mr. Cardoza. But I couldn't find it, so I took all my books out and then, at the bottom of my locker, I found this!"

She rattled the paper. "But how could someone get into your locker?" Mr. Cardoza asked patiently. "Don't you keep it locked?"

"I left my locker open for about ten minutes this morning so Heather could pick up a book I borrowed," Corrin explained. "Someone must have taken my report then. I didn't notice anything until just now. My report is gone and *this* was on top of my books!"

Mr. Cardoza took the yellow paper. He studied the two tiny black-inked figures curiously, then looked up at the class. "Does anyone know anything about this?" he asked. "Heather, did you see this paper in Miss Burns's locker this morning?"

Heather looked at Corrin and gulped. "Uh, no, I've never seen anything like that in my life. I . . . "

"The only place I've seen anything like it is on Kim Park's papers," snapped Corrin, cutting Heather off.

No one else moved or answered. Mr. Cardoza turned back to Corrin. "I'm sorry, Miss Burns, and I don't know what to do about this. If I were you, I'd concentrate on rewriting your paper and not on making foolish accusations. If I give you another day, can you rewrite your paper from your notes?"

Corrin shook her head. "I'll need at least two days."

Mr. Cardoza nodded. "If I give you two days, I will expect the best paper you've ever produced. Agreed?"

Corrin made a point of glaring at Kim, then nodded to Mr. Cardoza. She slipped into her desk, and Julie Anderson and Heather Linton leaned over to whisper encouragement.

"Miss Dixon," Mr. Cardoza looked at Meredith. "Am I still to receive your Shakespeare paper on Friday?"

"Yes, Mr. Cardoza. I've just finished *Hamlet.*"

"Excellent." He looked around at the rest of his class, the normal students, and cleared his throat. "Would everyone else please pass your papers forward?"

Meredith leaned toward Nicki. "Why would someone leave a yellow sheet of paper with a mark on it?" she whispered. "If someone really wanted Corrin's paper, which is crazy, why wouldn't they just take it?"

"Maybe someone just doesn't like Corrin," offered Christine.

"Do you?" crooned Laura. "I'm not wild about the girl, but I'd never take her paper."

"Okay," Christine grinned. "Maybe someone took it because they *hate* Corrin."

"Maybe someone is having trouble with English and

needed a paper so they could get ideas," offered Meredith thoughtfully. "And maybe someone has this idea, perhaps from another culture, that it's okay to take something if you leave something in its place."

"Are you saying Kim took Corrin's essay?" Nicki couldn't believe what Meredith was implying.

"What about the little Oriental symbols? You know Kim writes in Korean all the time."

"Yeah, but she's not so stupid as to take something and leave a calling card, for heaven's sake!" Nicki shook her head. "Besides, I just don't think she'd steal something. I don't think it is right to steal in *anyone's* culture."

"You don't know that it's not perfectly ordinary in Korea to borrow from someone," Meredith countered. "Maybe she thought taking Corrin's paper was a sort of compliment, and maybe she was planning to return it."

"Maybe that's what the writing means," offered Laura. "'Be back soon,' or something like that."

"If she wanted to take a good English paper, she'd take yours," pointed out Nicki, nodding to Meredith. "You're the only one who gets *A*s from Mr. Cardoza."

Christine cleared her throat. "Hello? Anyone listening? Has anyone considered that maybe Kim took it because she just doesn't like Corrin?"

Nicki looked over at Corrin, who was making faces at Kim's back. "I know for sure that Corrin doesn't like Kim."

"Well, are we going to help her or not?" Christine reminded her friends. "We said we were going to help Kim out."

"We were going to help her with English," said Meredith. "That was our promise."

"Maybe she needs our help in another way," Nicki suggested. "If she took the paper, we need to teach her that taking someone's paper is wrong. If she didn't do it, she'll need our help because it looks like Corrin is going to make her life pretty miserable at school."

"She can do it," whispered Meredith, who still hadn't forgotten the insults of last year.

"Okay, then," Nicki whispered as Mr. Cardoza finished stacking their research papers and walked over to the chalkboard. "Our fearless foursome will take on a new project after class. Meredith, why don't you and Laura ask Mr. Cardoza for a closer look at that yellow paper? Christine, you come with me and let's talk to Kim. Maybe we can solve this thing right away."

Christine and Nicki caught up with Kim after class. "Kim, we'd like to find out what happened to Corrin's research paper. Do you know anything about it?"

Talking to Kim wasn't easy. First of all, she was so shy she kept ducking her head and Nicki always found it hard to talk to people who wouldn't look her in the eye. "Look people in the eye," her parents always told her. "You'll look like you have confidence." Since both her parents were confident salespeople, Nicki figured eyeballing people was high on their list of priorities.

But Kim wouldn't stop walking down the hall or even look up, which didn't say much for *her* confidence. She didn't answer Nicki, so Christine plunged in: "Kim, we hope you're getting along okay here in school, and we want to make things easier for you. Where are you going, your locker?"

Kim kept her head down, but she nodded. Christine

smiled. "Okay, let's go to your locker."

Nicki didn't know how to begin. "Do you like America?" she stammered. "Is school here a lot like school in Korea?"

Kim had begun to unlock her lock, but she stopped twirling the combination long enough to look up and smile. "We go to school six days a week in Korea. Only five days here. Students must wear uniforms in Korea. And girls go to one school, boys to another. This," she looked up and nodded at the confusion around her, "is strange."

Christine and Nicki grinned at each other. Good! That was the most Kim had said since they had met her. As Kim continued to dial her combination, Nicki saw Meredith and Laura rushing over and waving the yellow piece of paper. Mr. Cardoza must have given it to them.

"I'm so glad you like school," Nicki smiled at Kim, who snapped the lock and opened the locker door. "We wanted to . . . " Nicki stopped in mid-sentence as Kim's locker opened. A pile of folded yellow papers fell out onto the floor.

Laura, Meredith, Christine and Nicki stood with their mouths open. Kim merely seemed bewildered, and she dug under a pile of papers still in her locker for her science book.

Meredith knelt by the papers on the floor and held the paper from Mr. Cardoza next to the pile. "It's the same kind of paper," she said slowly. "The same shade of yellow, the same thickness, the same everything."

"Kim," Nicki asked gently, "Are these your papers?"

Kim looked down at the floor. "My papers? My locker," she shrugged, "my papers." Then in Meredith's voice, "The same shade of yellow, the same thickness, the same everything."

Nicki felt horrible. The yellow papers were Kim's. Kim must have taken Corrin's research paper. She had practically admitted it.

"Sixty seconds till the bell," Meredith announced. Her inner clock was never wrong, so the girls snapped out of their shock. Before they left, Nicki took one of the yellow papers from the floor and asked Meredith for the paper from Corrin's empty folder. She didn't know what to do next.

The four girls were glum as they walked home.

"What should we do?" Nicki asked. "Should we tell a teacher that we think Kim took Corrin's essay?"

"Maybe we should just tell Corrin," Laura suggested. "It was her essay."

"If Corrin got in trouble, she probably deserved it," grumbled Meredith. "She was giving Kim a hard time the other day."

"Whenever one of us kids is in trouble at home, my dad always says, 'You're innocent until proven guilty!' " said Christine. Her father was the principal of Pine Grove Christian School, as well as the father of six, so Nicki guessed he had a lot experience with proving guilt. "In our house, it's hard to tell who did what, and believe me, my older brother and sister have tried to frame us lots of times for things we didn't do."

"Well, Kim needs someone to help her, that's for sure," Laura sighed. "I'd hate to be new in school and not have anyone to stick up for me." She smiled at the others. "Ya'll have been super, and I appreciate everything you've done."

Meredith and Nicki smiled at Laura, and Christine gamely threw an arm around her. "It's a pleasure to have you with us, kiddo," Christine grinned. "I never knew anyone who rode to school in a limo could be, you know, a real person."

Laura smiled. "Yeah, I'm a real person," she said softly, "and Kim is too. And I think we ought to help her."

"What if she took Corrin's paper?" Meredith said, looking down at the sidewalk. "Could we trust a friend like that?"

"Maybe she just doesn't understand," Christine answered. "We can work with her and teach her what's cool and what's not."

"Maybe our foursome needs to be a fivesome," Nicki thought out loud. "Okay, even if she took Corrin's paper, we'll stand by our promise to help her. Agreed?"

"Agreed," said Laura.

"Agreed," said Christine.

Meredith sighed. "Okay, I agree."

The next morning as the girls walked on to the school grounds, they noticed that the crowd of kids who usually hung around outside were streaming into the building. "Are we late?" Christine worried.

"No way," said Meredith without even checking her watch. "We've got at least ten minutes until the warning bell."

"Something's up," said Nicki, walking faster. "Let's check it out."

They followed the flow of students to the open area where the lockers were. At the center of the crowd was a wailing Corrin Burns.

"I'm cursed, I tell you," she was yelling at Mr. Padgett, the principal. "My research paper was stolen yesterday and today this *thing* has been painted on my locker. It's a curse! Someone is out to get me!"

Mr. Padgett was saying that curses were sheer nonsense, but someone was guilty of vandalism and he'd find out soon enough who it was, thank you very much. As he muttered about suspensions and detentions, those closest to the scene of the crime quickly walked away. Nicki and her friends squeezed into the gap.

On the door of Corrin's locker were the same Oriental figures they had seen on the yellow sheet of paper. But this time they had been painted boldly with black spray paint.

"Move on, everybody," Mr. Padgett boomed above the noise. "Everyone to your locker and then to homeroom."

In Mrs. Balian's homeroom, the rumors were flying fast and furious. "The curse of the dragon lady," whispered Natalie Martin to Jansen Moore. "It's some Kung-Fu thing."

"Three days of terrible, awful luck," moaned Holly Phillips to Michelle Vander Hagen. "Corrin says she's afraid to get out of bed tomorrow."

"Where'd the curse come from?" Jeff Jordan asked loudly. Twenty heads turned in his direction, then twenty pairs of eyes nodded silently toward the back of Kim Park, who sat quietly in the front row.

"This is ridiculous," Nicki snapped, hearing the comments around her. "How can anyone believe Corrin's story about a curse?"

"You know how rumors are," Meredith shrugged. "By the end of the day she'll be cursed with three *years* of bad luck."

"Or to have three *ears* growing out of her head," giggled Christine.

"That's all nonsense," Nicki mumbled, but she had to smile. Especially when Corrin came into the room and moved slowly toward her seat, pale and shaken, with Heather and Julie hanging onto her arms like any moment Corrin would breathe her last.

Corrin nodded weakly at her classmates and fluttered her lashes limply in Scott Spence's direction. She managed a weak glare at the back of Kim Park's head.

"I think I'm going to be sick," Laura chirped.

"I think I'm going to do something about this," Nicki decided. "It's silly for Kim to sit up there in the front row where people can do things behind her back."

Nicki walked up to the front of the room and crossed to Kim's desk. "Kim, why don't you come sit with us?" Nicki asked. "There's an extra seat over in our corner of the room."

Kim blushed, bowed her head and smiled up again. "This seat is not good?" she asked.

"No, Kim," Nicki answered, taking Kim's books off the desk. "This seat is *not* good. Come with me."

Kim followed and Nicki pointed out an empty desk against the wall just behind Christine. *Now,* Nicki thought, *if anyone makes faces in Kim's direction, at least she'll see what's going on.*

The bell rang, the announcements were given, the class stood to say the pledge. Mrs. Balian was busy grading papers at her desk as the class waited for the bell for first period to ring. Usually everyone huddled and talked quietly in little groups, but today Corrin was the center of attention.

"I don't really know if it's a curse," she now admitted in her nasal voice. "I supposed it could be just a weird coincidence."

"How can that symbol on your locker be just a coincidence?" Julie Anderson asked protectively. "Why was it on your locker?"

"Now that, I don't know," shrugged Corrin. "I don't know why anybody would have anything against me. But there are some really nasty, mean people in the world, people that aren't like us. I mean just over there . . . " she leaned toward her friends, then turned to sneak a look at Kim.

But like everyone else, Kim had been watching Corrin. When their eyes met, Kim opened her mouth and in Corrin's oboe voice said, "But there are some really nasty, mean people in the world."

Corrin slumped over in her chair in a dead faint.

5

After Corrin came around, waving and flailing her arms, Mrs. Balian wrote her a pass to go see the school nurse. "Tell her to let you go home," Mrs. Balian said simply. "Anyone who is sick enough to faint is sick enough to go home."

Corrin protested, putting her hand to her head and glancing over at Scott Spence. "But, Mrs. Balian, I'm okay now. I think I can make it through the day." She paused and sighed. "Especially if someone could help me carry my books."

"Hrmphfff," Michelle Vander Hagen's disgust showed on her face.

"No, Corrin, tell the nurse to let you go home," Mrs. Balian was firm and waved Corrin toward the door. "We'll see you tomorrow if you're feeling better."

Corrin dragged her feet toward the door. "Tomorrow! Under this curse, I'll probably be hit by a school bus! I won't live through tomorrow!"

"What an act!" groaned Meredith as the door closed.

"Do you think it was?" asked Laura, her eyes wide. "I've never seen anyone faint before except my grandmother. She faints any time there's a crisis, and Corrin's faint looked real to me."

"Maybe it was partly real and partly fake," Nicki

mused. "Maybe she was incredibly surprised to hear Kim answer in her own voice and to cover her shock, she pretended to faint."

"No one else seemed to notice Kim's little part in the drama," Christine pointed out. "Everybody was so busy trying to figure out if Corrin was cursed that no one but us was paying any attention to Kim."

"Maybe Corrin's fainting was part of the curse," added Laura. "You know, maybe the curse made her faint."

"You don't really believe she's cursed, do you?" Meredith elbowed Laura, hard. "That's impossible."

"We're forgetting someone," Nicki reminded them and pointed to Kim. Ever since Nicki had invited Kim to sit by them, she was always near the girls, watching and listening. Kim was watching again, her pretty dark eyes alert.

"Kim, do you know anything about a curse?" Nicki asked.

Kim shook her head.

Nicki pulled out a sheet of notebook paper and tried her best to imitate the two black Oriental figures they had seen on the yellow paper and on Corrin's locker. "Do you know what this means?"

Kim studied the figures for a moment, then shook her head. "Not Korean," she smiled. "Perhaps Chinese?"

"Chinese?" Meredith asked. "What does it mean?"

Kim smiled and raised an eyebrow. "I'm not Chinese. I am Korean."

"Sorry," Meredith muttered.

The bell rang and the girls gathered their books. "What do you think?" Nicki whispered to Meredith. "If she doesn't know what the sign means, she didn't write it."

"But what if she's lying?" Meredith protested. "She could be trying to throw us off the track."

Nicki shook her head. The mystery of the mark was as cloudy as ever, but she couldn't believe Kim would lie to her only friends.

Mr. Gilbert, the geography teacher, was full of surprises. "In order to give ourselves a full view of the world," he boomed in his lecture voice, "we're spending this hour in the library. I want you to choose a foreign country and prepare a five-minute oral report on it. These reports will be presented in class beginning tomorrow."

The entire class groaned. "Come on, it's not so bad," Mr. Gilbert said. "There's just one more thing. Everyone must choose a different country, so let me know which country you'd like to study. First come, first choice."

"Isn't this rather *sudden*?" asked Nicki, caught off guard. "I just spent tons of time in the library for English."

"Maybe Mr. Gilbert has a crush on the new librarian," Christine said, furiously batting her eyelashes. "Didn't you notice her name is *Miss* Phillips?"

"It's more likely Mr. Gilbert was too busy last night to prepare his lesson plans," added Meredith, the daughter of two professors. "The library is a *great* place for teachers to kill time."

"I have an idea!" Nicki snapped her fingers. "Maybe through our reports we can find out something about Corrin's mystery mark. We'll sign up right away and choose the Asian countries. Meredith, you choose China. Laura, why don't you take Taiwan? Christine, you take Japan, and I'll take Korea. Okay?"

"I was sort of hoping to study Paris," Laura sighed. "My mama says she'll take me there next summer if I do well in school."

"Paris isn't a country, it's a city in France," Meredith quickly corrected. "And Nicki's idea is good. Right?"

The girls nodded. Everyone, that is, except Kim, who softly asked, "What do I study?"

"Kim," Nicki paused, thinking. "Why don't you ask Mr. Gilbert if he'll let you study the United States?"

The girls split up in the library and Nicki brought the "K" volume of the encyclopedia to the table where she was working. Under "Korea" she skimmed the subheadings: history, population, geography, climate. Nothing about curses. Rats.

Scott Spence slid into the empty chair across from her. "Hi."

"Hi, yourself," Nicki replied, thinking of the looks she'd be getting if Corrin or Michelle Vander Hagen were around. "What country did you choose?"

"Canada."

"Why Canada?"

Scott shrugged. "I was going to study Newfoundland because I have a Newfoundland dog." He laughed and Nicki noticed his face turned slightly red. "But Newfoundland isn't a country. I found out it's a province in Canada."

Nicki couldn't stop a giggle. The librarian looked their way and Nicki lowered her voice a notch. "What's a Newfoundland dog?"

Scott flipped through the pages of his encyclopedia,

Volume "N." "Here," he pushed the book toward her.

A picture of the biggest, blackest, furriest dog in the world covered the page. "Wow! You have one of these?"

Scott smiled proudly. "You bet. Over 150 pounds of pure muscle and champion dog."

"What's his name?"

"Pine Grove's Valiant McArthur."

Nicki had to bit her tongue to keep from laughing. "All that name for one dog?"

"Of course." Mr. Gilbert walked by and Scott stopped talking for a moment to rustle some papers. "You don't give a dinky little name to a dog like McArthur."

"Is that what you call him? I mean, you don't go out and say, 'Here, Pine Grove's whatever-whoever-whenever.'"

"No, we call him Mack for short."

"That's a dinky little name," Nicki reminded him.

Scott leaned toward her. "Is a Mack truck a dinky little truck?"

Nicki shook her head and grinned. He had a point.

Miss Phillips walked by and they read their encyclopedias.

"What country did you choose?" Scott asked when the coast was clear.

"Korea."

"Why Korea?"

Nicki thought better of mentioning the mystery. "Because Kim's from Korea."

"Oh yeah?" Scott thought a moment. "She's really cute. Lots of the guys think so."

"Really?" Any of the other girls would kill to hear Scott say they were cute, but Nicki thought Kim would probably just be embarrassed.

"Yeah."

"Scott Spence told me he thought Kim was really cute," Nicki told Meredith, Laura and Christine after school as they stood by the lockers. "Should I tell her?"

"Oh, yes!" voted Laura. "That'd make my day."

"Maybe," said Christine. "Would it embarrass her?"

"Definitely not," muttered Meredith. "You'll only make her self-conscious."

"Well, she *is* cute," Nicki answered. "And more people would see it if she'd lift her head and be more self-confident. Maybe we could help her feel good about herself. We don't have to say that it's Scott Spence who thinks she's cute."

"*Who?*" Julie Anderson had overheard Nicki's words and she popped her head around the row of lockers like a jack-in-the-box. "Who does Scott Spence like?"

"Kim Park," answered Christine.

"I don't know that he *likes* her," Nicki explained, "but I guess he does, as a friend."

"He thinks she's a raving beauty," Laura smiled at Julie. "Isn't that wonderful?"

Julie took off and joined up with Heather Linton and Michelle Vander Hagen on the other side of the lockers. "Now you've done it, Laura," Meredith said. "The news will be everywhere in ten minutes."

"I know," Laura said, hugging her notebook to her.

"It could make things interestin'."

Nicki didn't know if "interesting" was quite the word to describe the next day. Corrin Burns was back in school, but she was dressed in black from head to toe. Black hat, black dress, black tights and black combat boots. *I like to dress a little on the funky side once in a while,* thought Nicki, *but even I've never come up with anything as downright weird as that outfit.*

As they waited for the tardy bell in homeroom, Jeff Jordan called out, "Hey, Corrin, what's with the black? Are you in mourning?"

"Of course, you ignoramus," she called over her shoulder. She turned back to the safety of her friends. "Some people are so lucky. They will never know how terrifying it is to live under a curse. I only hope it ends today. That dragon lady is the last person on earth I want to deal with!"

Heather Linton saw Kim Park come in. Heather put her fingers beside her eyes and stretched the skin outward. "Chink warning," Heather murmured. Corrin ducked under her hat and turned away. Julie Anderson made a gallant attempt to shield Corrin with her notebook while Heather held an oversized geography book over Corrin's face. "Hide me, hide me," Corrin squealed. "How could *anyone* say that girl is cute? I'll never understand it!"

"Hi, Kim," Nicki called, a little too brightly. "Come on over and sit down." Nicki noticed that Kim's lower lip quivered slightly as she made her way to her seat.

"If the dragon lady comes near you," Corrin was explaining loudly to anyone who would listen, her back to Kim and Nicki, "you have to raise two fingers in a 'V' and wiggle them, like this."

Corrin raised two fingers before her own wide eyes, then she whirled to face Kim. Fingers wriggling, she shrieked, "Curses to curses, dragon lady. Curses back to you!"

Kim's eyes filled with tears and she threw her hands over her face. "That's enough, Corrin," Nicki protested, noticing that several kids were either copying Corrin or giggling. "There's no such thing as a curse and Kim didn't put one on you."

"Oh, yeah, Nicki Holland?" The brim of Corrin's hat bobbed up and down. "We'll just see about that. Don't mess with things you don't understand. *You* just might get hurt!"

6

In English on Friday, Mr. Cardoza handed back the research papers. Nicki's paper on Margaret Mitchell had earned a *B+* and Laura got a *B* on Charlotte Brontë. "Please clean up the tear stains on your pages, Miss Cushman," Mr. Cardoza had written in his famous red ink pen.

Christine got a *C* on her cockatiel paper. "Ugh, it's bleeding," she moaned. "Just look at all that red ink." Across the top of her paper, Mr. Cardoza had scrawled, "Really now, is this great literature?" Christine was offended, "To my mother and her birds, this is great stuff."

"Now, I believe I need two additional papers," Mr. Cardoza reminded the class. "Miss Burns and Miss Dixon, are your papers ready?"

Corrin handed Mr. Cardoza a black folder. "It's all there," she said proudly. "The best thing I've ever done, just like you said."

Meredith was still digging through her book bag. "Miss Dixon?" Mr. Cardoza waited.

Meredith looked up, her eyes wide. "I can't find my paper," she stammered. "I know I had it here in my book bag. It has to be here somewhere!"

"I am growing tired of this disappearing paper theme," Mr. Cardoza remarked dryly. "Miss Dixon, you have until the end of the day to bring me your paper. Perhaps you will find it in your locker."

"Yes, sir," Meredith sat numbly, not moving.

"Meredith, where could you have left your paper?" Nicki whispered. "Do you want us to help you look for it?"

"There's no sense in looking. It's gone." Meredith's eyes were steely now. "Look what I found in my book bag." From her bag Meredith pulled out a folded sheet of yellow paper. She unfolded it carefully, but Nicki and the others knew what they would see inside: the mysterious mark of the curse.

If Corrin had been cursed, Nicki thought dryly, *she certainly was having better luck than anyone else on Friday.*

By the time the group was together in geography, Meredith was an emotional wreck. Corrin, who wouldn't have to give an oral report because she had the good fortune to faint the day it was assigned, was as cool as a cucumber.

Even more unlucky for Meredith, hers was the first name Mr. Gilbert called. *Was it just because he knew she'd be ready?* Nicki wondered. *Maybe being super-smart was sort of a curse in itself.* Meredith got up and gave a good five-minute summary of China, which wasn't easy because, as Meredith pointed out, China has more people and probably more history than any other nation on earth.

As she passed by Nicki on her way back to her seat, Meredith whispered: "And no, I didn't learn anything about curses or symbols. If that symbol is Chinese, it is one of thousands of Chinese figures in two or three dialects. And I still haven't found my research paper."

Meredith propped up her geography book and began trying to rewrite her paper on William Shakespeare and *Hamlet* from memory while Jansen Moore reported on

Australia in a fake and very poor Australian accent. "He's just trying to sound like Mel Gibson," Christine crinkled her freckled nose. "That's pitiful."

Nicki's name was called next. She shuffled her notes and walked to the front of the room, quickly running her tongue over the front of her teeth. Last year she had seen a guy give an oral report with a sprout of broccoli stuck to his front tooth. Nicki *never* wanted that to happen to her.

"I chose to do my report on South Korea because our new friend, Kim, is Korean," Nicki said, taking a deep breath. "The Koreans are a proud people. It is a country blending change with old traditions. The more common family names are Kim, Lee, Park, Chung and Han. A woman does not change her name when she is married."

Nicki looked up from her notes. Kim was smiling. Good. Nicki wanted to do a good job for her sake.

"Seoul, the capitol of South Korea, is a very modern city with subways, highways, taxis, hotels and the athletic centers of the 1988 Olympics. It has many fine restaurants.

"The people like to eat rice, mainly, and a dish made from pickled cabbage called kimchi. Food is usually eaten mixed together."

Nicki heard several "yucks" and looked up with a smile. "The food is very good," she assured the class. "In open air markets people can buy ducks, live chickens or even dogs."

Nicki wasn't quite prepared for the reaction.

"Gross!"

"That's awful!"

"Eating dogs!"

"Totally disgusting!"

Mr. Gilbert rapped a ruler on his desk. "Don't judge every culture by your own," he reminded them. "Remember that snails are a delicacy in France; ants, worms and beetles are considered fine foods in Africa."

"Ughhhhh!" everyone groaned.

"Those people aren't like us," Corrin Burns said airily. "Sometimes I think we're the only people in the world with any sense."

Mr. Gilbert frowned. "Perhaps they think it's a shame we aren't more like them," he said. "Nicki, please go on."

"My five minutes are almost up," Nicki said, grateful at least that the uproar had killed some time. "There are two important birthdays in the life of a Korean—the first and the sixtieth, when the cycle of active life is completed. Korea, and Koreans, are interesting."

Everyone applauded politely and Nicki sat down.

"Next," called Mr. Gilbert, "is Scott Spence reporting on Canada. Scott?"

Scott rolled his eyes, and reached for his notebook.

"Uh oh."

"What's wrong, Scott?" Mr. Gilbert asked.

"Don't tell me," Christine muttered. "His report is missing."

Scott held up his report. It wasn't missing, but someone had covered his notes with the now-famous mystery mark. Some kind of heavy black marker had totally covered Scott's work.

"Scott, is this some sort of trick to get out of giving your report?"

Scott shook his head, but no one noticed because

Corrin jumped out of her seat, two fingers raised and wriggling in that crazy sign. "It's the curse!" she shouted. "It's been passed on to you, Scott! Look out! For the next three days I'd stay home! She did it to you! The dragon lady!"

After Meredith took her quickly written Shakespeare report to Mr. Cardoza, she met Christine, Laura, Nicki and Kim by their lockers. "Listen, let's get together tonight," Nicki suggested. "Whose mother will let us come over?"

Christine rolled her eyes. "My mother wouldn't care, but with all the noise at my house we wouldn't get anything done."

Meredith shook her head. "Tonight is supposed to be my night at my dad's apartment, and he's not up to having a bunch of girls over. But he wouldn't care if I went somewhere."

"My mom and dad probably wouldn't mind," Nicki offered, "but Mom's showing a house tonight and Dad's trying to sell insurance to some new neighbors."

"Well, then, it's settled," smiled Laura. "My mom and I would just love to have ya'll over. Kim, are you sure you can come?"

Kim smiled, and a pretty flush shone through her pale skin. "I will ask," she nodded. "This is a slumber party? We will sleep?"

"Sort of," Meredith smiled. "We'll talk a lot and sleep a little. It'll be fun."

"Mother will send the car to pick you all up," Laura smiled again. "Just be ready at six o'clock."

Kim waved goodbye as she went to meet her bus, and

the four other girls gathered their books to walk home.

Suddenly an angry voice destroyed the after-school silence: "I'm getting just a little tired of this!" Nicki and the others sprinted past three rows of lockers until they saw Scott Spence scowling. "It was bad enough that my report was ruined, but now I'll probably have to pay to have my locker repainted!"

Scott's locker was decorated with the mystery mark, spray painted, probably, and in a hurry, too, because a messy drip was even now running onto the locker beneath Scott's.

"Did you see anyone come by here?" Nicki asked him.

"School's been out for ten minutes, Nicki," Scott reminded her. "*Everybody's* been by here."

"Does anyone see any other clues?" Meredith asked.

Aside from the usual trash left at the end of the day, there was nothing. "Well, Kim was with us," Laura smiled. "So we know *she* didn't do it."

"No, she had left us," Meredith pointed out. "She has been gone about four minutes, and this paint *is* fresh."

"Scott, this mark was also on your report, right?" Nicki asked. "Did you leave your notebook around at any time today or yesterday? How could someone have marked your report?"

Scott ran his fingers through his hair, thinking. "That's crazy, Nicki. All of us leave our notebooks out sometimes. We always stash them on an empty table at lunch. And just this morning I left my notebook on the sidewalk outside while we were riding Jeff Jordan's skateboard."

"Why don't you keep your notebook with you?" asked Christine.

Scott shrugged. "You just don't think that someone

would want to steal your homework." He laughed. "Anybody'd be crazy to steal mine."

Nicki smiled at his joke. "Anyway, it's a shame about your locker. Mr. Padgett is going to be upset that it happened again."

"Whoever did it is gone now," said Scott, carefully opening his locker without touching the wet paint. "Wait— here's something else!"

On top of Scott's books and rolled-up gym towel was a folded sheet of yellow paper—identical, it seemed, to those the girls had already seen in Kim's locker. It was also identical to the papers left for Meredith and Corrin.

Scott carefully unfolded the paper. In the center of the page was the mystery mark, carefully drawn, but on his paper there were also two words written in block letters: DOG MEAT.

"Dog meat?" Scott read. "What in the world does *that* mean?"

"It could mean that *you're* dog meat," answered Christine. "My brother Tommy says that every time he threatens my little brothers. Does someone want to beat you up?"

"It could have something to do with *eating* dog meat," said Meredith thoughtfully. "Sort of like saying to someone, 'Go eat nails.' Maybe in another culture they say, 'Go eat a Chihuahua.' "

Meredith leaned to whisper in Laura's ear: "Maybe a certain young lady got embarrassed because Scott said she was cute and . . . "

"You can't believe that," Laura gasped. She whispered fiercely: "Would you get mad if Scott said *you* were cute?"

"Maybe—if I were shy and the whole school was talking about me," Meredith whispered back.

"Maybe the letters mean something else. The letters could be jumbled together or in code." Nicki took the paper from Scott. "Do you mind if we take this? We're all staying at Laura's tonight. We're sort of investigating all the strange happenings around school."

Scott grinned at Nicki. "Investigators, huh?"

Nicki blushed and noticed the other girls were giving her "since-when-did-you-two-get-friendly?" looks.

"Yeah, you could say that. We're trying to help Kim get adjusted here, too."

Scott frowned. "You don't believe Corrin's story about a curse?"

Meredith snapped her gum. "Corrin's crazy and she's already got too many other people believing her nutty tales. Of course there's no such thing as a curse. Someone's just making trouble, that's all."

Scott closed his locker. "Well, good luck, Nicki Holland and company. Let me know if I can do anything to help."

As Scott walked away, Laura called out a warning: "Just be careful, Scott. You found the mystery mark, and there are still two and a half days of the curse left!"

"Laura, you really don't believe in the curse, do you?" Meredith asked. "I mean, I found one of those mystery mark papers in my bookbag and no matter what happens, I refuse to believe there are three days of bad luck out there waiting for me."

"No," Laura shook her head so that her blond curls danced. "I don't think I believe in a curse. 'Specially not one from Kim Park. But someone has their heart set on making trouble—for Corrin, for Scott and for you. Doesn't that worry you just a little bit? I'd be scared speechless."

"Nothing will happen," Meredith snapped. "It's the weekend and everyone's out of school. So far everything bad has happened at school, and we'll be home this weekend." She lowered her voice so that only Nicki could hear. "Plus, we'll have Kim Park with us. Nothing else can happen."

After the girls had been picked up by Laura's chauffeur and fed hand-tossed pizza by the Cushman's cook, they relaxed in Laura's room. Or perhaps "suite" would be a better description. The bedroom had an adjoining sitting room with two couches, a table, television, stereo and rowing machine. A bathroom off to the other side was bigger than Nicki's bedroom.

"This place is fantastic," Meredith sighed when they all trooped upstairs after eating. "This is bigger than my bedrooms at my mom's and dad's put together!"

"I'd shave my head for this room," Christine said, twirling around in the spaciousness. "I can't believe it! I've shared a room with at least one sister for as long as I can remember. All of this is for just you?"

Laura looked a little embarrassed. "There's really just me and mother. My sister April goes to boarding school in Vermont, so when she's home she stays in the guest room downstairs."

Nicki smoothed a tiny wrinkle out of the peach-flowered chintz bedspread and looked around. "Where's Kim? Did we lose her?"

Kim stepped out of Laura's cavern of a closet. "I'm sorry," she stammered. "I've never seen a room just for clothes and shoes."

"Closet, Kim," Meredith instructed. "That's just a closet, but that's probably the biggest one in Pine Grove."

Laura giggled. "My mother's is bigger."

The girls laughed, but stopped quickly when the soft voice and gardenia fragrance of Mrs. Virginia Louise Cushman floated into the room. "I'm so glad you all have come," she said gently, her peaches and cream complexion blending perfectly with Laura's peach chintz furnishings. "Nicki, it's really a pleasure to meet you again. Laura, can I have the pleasure of meeting your other friends?"

Laura introduced Meredith, Christine and Kim, and Mrs. Cushman graciously shook each of their hands. "Well, girls, I'm going to retire early tonight," she smiled. "If there's anything at all you need, please let Mrs. Perkins know."

Nicki remembered her manners. "Thank you, Mrs. Cushman, for having us over," Nicki said. "You have a lovely home."

Everyone else murmured their agreement and Mrs. Cushman smiled. "Thank you, Nicki," she said. "You are such nice girls."

A faint scent of gardenia lingered in the air after she left, but the spell was broken when Laura grabbed a pillow from her bed and ran toward her sitting room. "Last one to the meeting has to keep notes," she called.

Two hours later, no one had taken any notes, but each girl had filled a notebook-paper page of doodles. It was a little difficult to discuss the mystery in front of Kim, whom Meredith kept referring to as "Suspect Number One." Nicki didn't really believe Kim was guilty of stealing, lying and vandalism, but somehow the mystery did seem to revolve around her.

"Maybe we should set some goals," Nicki said. "We're getting nowhere by just sitting around."

"Right," said Meredith. "And since I'm nearing the first deadline on my science project, I think we should test the scope of Kim's vocal mimicry."

"Kim, is that okay with you?" asked Laura gently.

Kim smiled and nodded. "I want to help my friends."

"Get comfortable," Meredith told her, so Kim settled back on the couch and tucked her legs under her.

"Okay, experiment," she said.

The girls said various words and phrases to hear how Kim would answer. Christine tried her Irish accent, modeled on her Aunt Milly. Kim answered, and it sounded not like Aunt Milly but exactly like Christine imitating Aunt Milly.

Laura smiled and whispered, "Do my mother."

Kim opened her mouth and they all heard Mrs. Cushman saying again, "Thank you, Nicki. You are such nice girls." Her words were so much like Mrs. Cushman's they could almost smell the gardenia perfume.

Laura shivered. "That's spooky."

Meredith's father had taught her how to speak an old English dialect, so she began reciting Chaucer: "Whan that Aprill with his shoures soote, The droghte of March hath perced to the roote . . . "

Kim sounded the poem back, word for word, exactly as Meredith had said it.

"That's amazing," Nicki said. "I can turn my back on you two and not know which one of you is talking."

"There is one final test," Meredith said calmly. She turned on the television and pressed the controls until she found a news broadcast.

"This is Dan Rather with a special report," said Dan Rather.

Meredith looked at Kim. "Can you do that?"

Kim closed her eyes and said in her own voice: "This is Dan Rather with a special report." Her presentation was similar, but her voice simply didn't have the depth she needed to imitate a man.

"That's the catch," said Meredith, pulling a pencil from her notebook. "Kim's voice isn't low enough to imitate a man's. She can do women and children perfectly, but apparently not men."

Nicki smiled at Kim. "Hey, Kim, can we play a little guessing game?"

Kim raised an eyebrow. "Guessing game?"

"Yes. You say something, anything, that you've heard people say and we'll try to guess who said it. Okay?"

Kim nodded and closed her eyes to think. "Okay." She took a deep breath. "Jeff Jordan, isn't this your third tardy this week?"

"I got it! Mrs. Balian!" Christine grinned. "That's unreal!"

Kim nodded and closed her eyes again. "If I don't see some action around here immediately, there will be a new list of detentions for next week!"

Even though she was imitating a man, there was no mistaking the principal's hurried accent. The girls giggled. "Mr. Padgett!"

Kim nodded. "I must think of someone harder." She closed her eyes and thought. Then she whispered, "Rats! Paint on my fingers!"

Nicki looked at Meredith. Meredith looked at Christine. Christine shook her head and looked toward Laura, whose eyes were as big as saucers.

"Kim, we don't know who that is," Laura said. "Who had paint on their fingers?"

Kim shook her head. "I don't know. I was in the water

closet and heard the voice. I couldn't see who spoke."

"Water closet?" Christine was puzzled.

"Restroom," Meredith translated.

"Did they whisper, just like you did?" Nicki asked.

"Just the same."

"Was there anyone in the bathroom when you came out?" Christine asked.

"No, no one."

"Did you see anything?" Nicki pressed.

"Nothing." Kim looked a little frightened.

Christine smiled at her reassuringly. "It's okay, Kim. No big deal. But when did this happen?"

Kim thought, then nodded. "I remember. Yesterday, after school. We said goodbye, I went to water closet, I mean restroom, and then to my bus. Yesterday."

Meredith looked at Nicki, and Nicki could almost see Meredith's mind beginning to work. Had Kim overheard the mysterious troublemaker or was she trying to throw them off the track of what had become an incredible mystery?

"Time to take a break," Christine called. She was getting restless. "Let's watch the movie I rented."

"Okay," Nicki said, "but after the movie we've got to set another goal. We promised Scott we'd work on this 'dog meat' clue."

The girls were glad to take a break, so for the next two hours they howled their way through a silly movie about a crime-solving detective and his Chinese pug. Kim cracked them up when she unexpectedly imitated the yowling of the dog perfectly.

Laura called down to the kitchen from the intercom

in her room and soon the housekeeper brought up a gigantic bowl of hot, buttered popcorn. "This is the life," Christine crowed. "Don't you think your mom might want to adopt me? My parents would never miss me."

When the movie was over and all that remained of the popcorn was a few unpopped kernels, the girls settled down to unravel the second part of the mystery.

"DOG MEAT—what does it mean?" Meredith asked. She looked at Kim. "Does anyone have any idea?"

Kim looked bewildered.

"Laura, do you have a Scrabble game?" Nicki asked.

"Sure," Laura replied. "Let me get it."

When Laura brought her Scrabble game, Nicki turned the game board upside down and then took the letters D O G M E A T out and placed them on the board. "What could you spell with this?" she asked aloud.

The girls began pushing and pulling the letters into different combinations. "DOG MEAT could also mean GOD TEAM or DOG MATE," Nicki announced. "That's silly."

"How about this?" Laura asked, excited. She spelled AT DOME G. "Is there a dome anywhere around here?"

"Not that I know of," Nicki shrugged. "I don't think that's it."

"How about GET A MOD?" asked Christine, pulling the letters into position. "Or GET A DOM?"

"Could it have something to do with a jewelry robbery?" asked Meredith. "I can spell TOAD GEM. Is there a famous diamond around here called the Toad Gem?"

Laura giggled. "If it were the color of a toad, it would be an emerald. I don't think there are any famous toady emeralds around school."

"Oooo, this is scary," Nicki said, moving Scrabble letters around. "How about MET G D.O.A.?"

"What does that mean?" Laura crinkled her nose.

"Someone with the initial G was met at the hospital dead on arrival—D.O.A.," Nicki explained. "I've seen little notes like that on my dad's desk when he's settling someone's life insurance policy."

"I don't think there is a message in code," Meredith sat up, stretching. "And I'm so tired my brain is turning to mush. Anyone for a late night creature feature?"

Somewhere during *Godzilla's Attack on the Amazon Women,* everyone dozed off. Except Nicki. She couldn't help feeling they were staring at something important and had somehow missed it.

8

At ten o'clock the next morning, Mrs. Perkins gently shook her shoulder. "Nicki, there's a telephone call for you. You can take it on the extension in Laura's bedroom, if you like."

Nicki had fallen asleep on one of the couches of Laura's sitting room, and she had to step over Kim and Meredith who were sleeping on the floor. She lifted the extension. "Hello?" She struggled to keep her eyes open.

"Nicki, this is Scott Spence. I'm sorry to bother you at Laura's."

"Scott?" Nicki was awake instantly. What in the world did he want at ten o'clock on Saturday morning? Nicki could feel herself blushing, and she was glad the other girls were asleep.

"Nicki, the curse has struck again. Mack is gone. Vanished into thin air," Scott sounded worried. "Dog meat, remember? Do you think that had something to do with Mack?"

"Wait a minute, slow down. Who's Mack?" Her brain felt cloudy, still fogged by sleep, Godzilla and late night giggles.

"McArthur, my dog. Remember?"

"Of course, now I remember. I'm sorry. What do you mean he vanished? Did you see him disappear?"

"I put him out this morning like I always do and when I called him to come in, he wasn't in the back yard. He was gone. It's the second day of the curse and he's gone."

"Now, wait a minute, Scott. Did you check the fence? Could he have dug under the fence?"

"No, I checked."

"Did you leave a gate open?"

"No. The gate was closed and latched."

"Could someone have stolen him?"

"Most people are too afraid of him to come near him because he's so big. I've never had anyone even come up to the gate before."

"But could someone have stolen him? Was the gate locked?"

Scott thought a minute. "No, the gate wasn't locked. And I guess someone *could* have taken him, because even though he looks like a big bear, he's really as friendly as a puppy. Mack likes everybody."

Nicki looked over at Kim, who was still asleep. At least Nicki knew Kim didn't take Scott's dog.

"Do you think it's the curse, Nicki? Did you guys figure anything out last night?"

"Come on, Scott," Nicki whispered because the other girls were beginning to stir, "you don't really think a *curse* lifted your dog out of your yard, do you?"

"No, but maybe the curse boils down to three days of bad luck, and my terrible luck happens to be that my dog got stolen! Do you think that's what DOG MEAT means?" Scott was really getting upset. "Do you think Kim Park took my dog? You said they eat dogs in Korea. That note said DOG MEAT."

"Scott, that's dumb," Nicki said. "Besides, Kim is here with me. She isn't eating your dog."

"I'm going to call the police."

"Okay, if it'll make you feel better, go ahead. But maybe Mack just ran away. Maybe there are just too many coincidences and you're feeling spooked. Mac will probably be home in time for supper."

Scott was calmer now, and he hung up after agreeing to call again if anything else happened. Nicki looked around the room where her friends were waking. Kim was sitting up, calmly watching Laura brush her hair its daily 100 strokes.

Were they wrong about the latest puzzle? Could DOG MEAT really mean dog meat, as in dog hamburger? Nicki suddenly felt very sorry she had ever mentioned food in her report on Korea.

Who was that?" Christine grinned. "Was it who I think it was?"

"It was Scott Spence," Nicki said, dropping into an overstuffed chair. "His dog is mysteriously missing and he thinks the curse has something to do with it."

Meredith looked at Kim, then back to Nicki. "Well, at least we know Suspect Number One had nothing to do with it. His dog is just probably out for a walk."

Nicki glared at Meredith for making the crack about Suspect Number One right in front of Kim, then she settled back to think. "Scott thinks someone might be out there *eating* his dog."

"Oh, I'm going to be sick," Christine groaned.

"It's just the popcorn kernels you insisted upon eating," Meredith remarked. "Now you have tiny pebbles in your stomach."

Nicki sat up, bright-eyed. "Why don't we go over to Scott's and look around?"

Laura grabbed Nicki's big toe and pulled it playfully. "Is there something you're not telling us? Do you like Scott Spence or something?"

"No more than anyone else," Nicki grinned, reaching for her overnight bag. "Let's get going. Get dressed and we'll go to Scott's and look around."

Mrs. Cushman was kind enough to provide breakfast and the limo driver for the girls. "I almost feel like we're real private eyes," Christine said as they rode along, munching on doughnuts. "Our own car! Is there any place else we need to go? To the mall? To the beach?"

"Come back down to earth," Meredith reached over Christine for another doughnut. "After we go to Scott's, I've got to get home. Dad will be upset if I don't spend any of my weekend with him."

"I need to get home, too," Kim offered softly. "My mother is ill and was very kind to let me come last night."

The girls were silent for a moment. "How is your mother?" asked Laura.

Kim smiled. "She is weak, but waiting. Soon the hospital will call with a kidney, and then my mother will go to hospital for the operation."

"Is your dad working?" Christine asked.

Kim nodded. "My father is a nuclear engineer and works for a company nearby. We came here to Pine Grove to be near my father's work, but we are a long way from the hospital where my mother will have her surgery. We only hope that when the time comes, we can afford to fly my mother to the hospital where she will have surgery. Many expenses." Kim shook her head.

The limo pulled up outside Scott's house in Kings' Grant. It was a large housing development. In fact, lots of kids from Pine Grove Middle School lived there, including Nicki, Christine and Meredith—when she was staying with her mom, at least. Scott was sitting on his front lawn, an empty leash in his hand.

"It's no use," he said as the girls walked up. "I've been up and down three different streets and I haven't seen anything of Mack."

Nicki looked at the house. Everything seemed normal. "Can we look around? Laura, why don't you and Kim ask the neighbors if they saw anything? Christine, you check the front, and Meredith and I will check the backyard and the fence."

She caught herself giving orders and blushed. "Sorry," she said. "I don't mean to be bossy. I'm just used to telling my little brother and sister what to do."

"It's okay," Scott said, standing up. "Come on, I'll show you the back yard."

The back yard was surrounded by a chain link fence, which meant that anyone could have seen Mack at any time of the day, Nicki noted. Perhaps someone had been admiring Mack for some time and simply had stolen him.

"Are Newfoundlands expensive?" she asked Scott.

"Usually," Scott answered. "I know, someone might have taken him to sell him. My dad even said that maybe someone stole Mack to use him in illegal dog fighting. But Mack wasn't aggressive. He isn't the fighting type, no matter how big he is."

Meredith had been walking along the edge of the fence. "There aren't any holes under the fence where he could have dug himself out," she reported. "There aren't any holes in the fence, either."

"I didn't see any footprints in the flower beds," Christine said.

Scott grinned. "Did you expect to find some?"

Christine shrugged. "Policeman always look for footprints in flower beds. But your flower beds are covered in mulch, and they don't show footprints."

"Neither does thick Florida grass," Nicki bit her lip thoughtfully. "What time did you let Mack out this morning?"

"He wanted out at 7:30, then I went back to bed," said Scott.

"Is that the time you usually let him out?"

"On school days I let him out at 6:30 when I get up," Scott said. "But everyone in my family sleeps in on Saturday."

"Do you usually let him out on Saturdays at 7:30?" Nicki asked.

Scott thought. "I guess so. Mack likes to get out early. That's pretty much our Saturday routine around here."

Meredith had a few more questions. "Does Mack have any enemies? Does he bark and disturb the neighbors? Has he ever bitten anyone?"

Scott shook his head. "Never. Everyone loves Mack. That's why it's so unbelievable that anyone would take him."

Laura and Kim returned from visiting the neighbors. "No one saw anything unusual," Laura reported. "No one was up before eight o'clock, except two little kids across the street and they were watching cartoons."

"I guess we should go now," Nicki told Scott. "We hope Mack comes back, but if this has anything to do with the so-called 'curse,' we'll figure it out soon." She frowned slightly. "I hope."

Laura asked the limo driver to take Kim home first. She lived in Levitt Park Apartments and the girls were all a little curious to know more about her.

"Won't you come in?" she asked when the car pulled

up by her apartment. Nicki hesitated, but Christine and Laura readily accepted. "Sure," Christine practically bounded out of her seat.

Kim knocked on the door, and a smiling man opened it. "Ah, Kim," he smiled and opened the door wider. "Please ask your friends to come in."

"I am Park Sang Soo," he said in the Korean way of placing his last name first. "It is great happiness to meet friends of Kim. My wife, Yoo Kyung, is pleased to meet you, too."

A lovely woman in a perfectly white dress sat on the couch and nodded gently toward the girls. "My mother does not speak English," Kim explained. She spoke to her mother in Korean, then smiled at her guests. "Would you like to have some tea?"

"I don't know about this," Meredith whispered to Nicki, but Nicki elbowed her. "Say yes," Nicki nodded respectfully to Kim's mother while whispering to Meredith. "It would be rude to say no."

The girls removed their shoes at the door and sat on a straw mat in front of a low table. Kim gave each girl a tea cup, and her father poured a green tea. Christine caught Laura's eye. "This had better be good," her look said, but when she tasted, it was.

When they had finished their tea and their polite conversation with Kim's parents, the girls went into Kim's bedroom. Instead of a normal bed, Kim slept on a pallet made of what looked like satin and silk. It was beautifully embroidered and rolled up for convenience when not in use.

"This is beautiful!" Laura exclaimed, rubbing her hand over a white satin coverlet. "Look at this beautiful embroidery!"

Kim smiled proudly. "My mother made it. She makes beautiful things."

"She must be very talented," Meredith remarked, looking at the quilt.

"Her name, Yoo Kyung, means 'delightful star,'" Kim smiled. "I honor her as my mother."

"I guess I honor my mother too," Christine said, thoughtfully. "With six kids, she deserves it."

"With six children, she needs it," smiled Kim. Her unexpected joke caught the girls by surprise.

"Kim, you have a sense of humor!" said Meredith.

"Is that surprising?" Kim asked. "Cannot Suspect Number One be funny?"

10

As the limo pulled away from Kim's apartment, Nicki, Laura, Meredith and Christine were more than a little embarrassed. Just because Kim was from another country didn't mean she was stupid, Nicki realized. And Kim had known all along that they suspected her of being behind the strange happenings at school. Yet, she didn't blame them and seemed to be as interested in solving the mystery as they were.

"Kim didn't do any of it," Nicki told the others flatly. "In order to find the guilty person, you must first establish that he or she had a motive and an opportunity to commit the crime. Kim has no motive. Plus, she didn't have a chance to take Scott's dog. She was with us."

"She looked like a good suspect for a while," Meredith said. "She had a locker full of yellow papers; she can write an Asian language; and Corrin Burns is so prejudiced Kim has every right to be mad at her. She had a reason to be mad at Scott, too, if she was embarrassed because everyone was saying that he thinks she's cute."

"That is crazy," Laura interrupted. "Anyone, including Kim, would be flattered if Scott liked them. Kim didn't have a motive for anything. I don't even think she holds anything against Corrin."

"Corrin has done nothing but make Kim's life miserable," Christine said, looking out the window. "Corrin yelled at her on the first day of school, calls her 'dragon lady'

68

and still does that weird stuff with her fingers."

"And her friends give a 'chink alert' whenever Kim walks by," Laura added. "That's terrible."

"Everyone knows Corrin is prejudiced," Nicki said. "Meredith, remember last year when she called you . . . "

"I remember," Meredith interrupted. "You don't have to remind me."

"Corrin's always been weird about stuff like that," Nicki went on. "It's one of the ways she gets attention. I can't believe how many people take her seriously."

"Okay, so if Kim isn't the guilty party, then we can trust her, right?" Meredith pulled out a sheet of paper. "And she gave us a couple of clues we ought to track down."

"That's right—the voice in the bathroom," Nicki remembered.

"We couldn't recognize it because it was whispered, but it was just one voice and not two," Meredith gestured with her pencil. "And it was a girl—unless a boy was sneaking into the girls' bathroom."

"That's too risky," Christine said. "No boy I know would do it."

"Then we know our culprit is a girl," Nicki said. "And we think she is acting alone."

"Practically every girl in our class had the same chance to commit the crime as every other girl," Christine thought aloud. "Maybe we should think about motives first."

"Okay—who would want to hurt Corrin Burns, and why?" Nicki asked.

"Michelle Vander Hagen might be jealous," Laura noted. "I've noticed that she doesn't like Corrin's flirting with Scott Spence."

Christine snapped her fingers. "Michelle Vander Hagen doesn't like being less than perfect, either. Didn't the voice in the bathroom complain because there was paint on her fingers?"

Meredith wrote MICHELLE V. HAGEN on the sheet of notebook paper.

"Heather Linton and Julie Anderson are Corrin's best friends," Meredith remarked.

"Would one of them want to hurt her?" Christine asked.

"Maybe, if they were secretly jealous or mad. Plus, since they're close to her, they'd know how to really get to her."

"Okay," Nicki pointed to the paper, "write them down, too."

"We know Kim didn't do it," sighed Laura. "Meredith, can we be sure that *you* didn't do it?"

"What?" Meredith was shocked.

"Corrin and you had that big run-in last year and I'm just making sure you don't have it in for Corrin Burns."

Meredith's eyes flashed. "If Corrin Burns gets into trouble, it will be because of her own ignorance, not mine," she retorted. "I didn't do it."

"Meredith didn't have an opportunity, either," said Christine, watching with interest. "She was with us when Scott's locker was painted and when the dog disappeared."

"Fine," Laura said simply.

"There's another name we ought to add to the list, then," Nicki said. "Write down Corrin Burns."

Christine was puzzled. "Why would Corrin Burns

steal her own paper and paint her own locker?"

"Why would she pick on Scott Spence when she practically drools on the boy?" asked Laura.

Nicki shrugged. "I don't know. But Meredith just said that Corrin's troubles might come out of her own ignorance. And she's a girl, and she had opportunity . . . "

"To steal her own paper?" Laura's eyes were wide.

"Sure. She got an extra two days to do her paper, didn't she? Just write her name down."

So by the time the limo driver pulled up outside Christine's house, the list read:

Suspects:	Motive:	Opportunity:
Michelle V. Hagen	*jealousy?*	*yes/maybe*
Heather Linton	*?*	*yes/maybe*
Julie Anderson	*?*	*yes/maybe*
Corrin Burns	*ignorance*	*yes/maybe*

11

Nicki found Scott Spence leaning against her locker on Monday morning. "Scott, did Mack come home?"

Scott grinned. "He came home yesterday."

Nicki opened her locker. "I told you he just got out somehow."

"No, Nicki, I don't think he just got out."

Nicki stopped, puzzled. "Why not?"

Scott looked grim. "When Mack came home, he was wearing *this* around his neck."

Scott took a bright yellow handkerchief from his jacket pocket. Someone had inked the mystery mark on to cotton material.

"What is this?" Nicki took the kerchief, surprised.

"Wow!" Meredith, Christine and Laura walked up. "Did you find that in your locker, Scott?"

"No, it was around Mack's neck when he finally came home yesterday."

"Was he hurt?" Christine asked.

"No," Scott shook his head. "Whoever took Mack took good care of him as far as I can tell. But why would someone take him at all? He's not an easy dog to take care of. He eats four or five times as much as other dogs. And if someone had him inside a house . . . " Scott grinned. "Mack eats coffee tables for breakfast."

"It would serve them right," Nicki said, still fingering the kerchief. "Someone is definitely sending you a message, though. And how did they get this symbol on this cotton material? This isn't paint exactly. It looks more like India ink."

"What's India ink?" Scott asked.

"It's special ink that won't run it if gets wet," Nicki explained. "And usually it's sold in bottles. To use it you have to dip an old-fashioned pen into the ink. My music teacher makes me write my compositions with it."

"That is how they make the figures so perfectly," said Kim. "It is hard to write in Chinese or Korean with a ball-point pen. Oriental figures are thin in some places, thick in others."

"There's one way to test it." Meredith took the kerchief from Nicki and walked to the water fountain. She wet the material, then rubbed the inked figures together. "It's not running," she said. "It must be India ink."

"Wait a minute," Nicki fumbled through her notebook and took out a yellow sheet of paper. "This is the paper Mr. Cardoza gave us—the one Corrin found in her locker." Nicki walked to the water fountain and splashed a few drops on the black writing.

"That's India ink, too," she smiled. "It isn't running, either."

"So our culprit writes with an old-fashioned pen dipped in India ink," mumbled Christine.

"Who could that be?" asked Laura. "Are we looking for a musician or an artist?"

"It could still be anyone," said Nicki, drying the yellow paper with the kerchief. "You can buy the pens at any stationery store, and India ink isn't hard to find, either." She smiled at Scott. "But at least Mack's back and you don't have to worry about him being dog meat."

Scott laughed. "Yeah, that's a relief. And you can keep the kerchief. Right now I'd do anything to help you catch whoever is doing this."

Nicki grinned. "Well, there's a place we have to investigate now, and I don't think you'll want to come."

"Where?" Scott asked.

Christine giggled. "The girls' water closet!"

Meredith crinkled her nose as Christine dug through trash in the girls' restroom. "Do you *know* what kind of germs are in there?"

"It's okay. This can't be worse than cleaning my brother's room," Christine said, pulling wet paper towels off her freckled arms. "I've had to do it for a month now."

"Christine Kelshaw," Nicki said. "What did you do this time?"

"Nothing much," said Christine as she washed her hands. "I only sprayed him with a can of shaving cream while his date was waiting in the living room." She giggled. "It was worth it, though. He deserved it after calling me that name."

"What name did he call you?" asked Laura, wide-eyed.

"Promise you won't ever call me that?"

"Sure." They all nodded.

"Christine Listerine. For that he deserved a face full of shaving cream."

"There's nothing here," Meredith leaned against the wall. "The custodians must have cleaned up over the weekend."

"If you had paint on your fingers, what would you do?" asked Nicki.

"Wash my hands," replied Kim. "Whoever was speaking was standing by the sink. I heard water running."

Nicki stood by the sink. "There's nothing here," she said, looking around. "No smudges, no fingerprints, nothing."

Just then the door opened and Michelle Vander Hagen walked in. "Oh . . . " she looked a little startled. "Hi. You guys aren't smoking in the bathroom, are you?"

"No," Nicki answered, watching Michelle carefully. "Just looking around."

"Good," Michelle answered. "I heard just *breathing* someone else's smoke will give you wrinkles." Michelle walked to the mirror, tossed her head at her reflection, and gave the mirror a practice smile. Her eyes darted quickly over the sink.

"Lose something, Michelle?" asked Christine.

"No," Michelle answered, shaking her golden hair down her back. "Nothing at all. Just wanted to make sure you guys were telling the truth. I'd hate to smell like cigarette smoke all day long."

The door closed and Michelle was gone. "Of all the nerve," Christine fumed. "Thinking we were smoking!"

"What if Michelle came in here for the same reason we did?" asked Meredith. "What if *she* was making sure she didn't leave any fingerprints, smudges or paint cans?"

Nicki bit her lip. "What if?"

12

At lunch the girls decided to be honest with Kim.

"At first, Kim," Nicki began, "we thought you might have something to do with what's been going on. But when Scott's dog was dognapped while you were with us, we knew you couldn't be involved."

Kim looked down at her lunch tray. "Why would you think of me?"

"It was the yellow papers," said Christine, opening her milk carton. "Your locker was full of yellow papers and you said they were yours. Why did you say that?"

Kim shook her head. "They were in my locker. I supposed someone gave them to me. That would make them mine, would it not?"

"But how could someone put them in your locker? Does someone have your locker combination?" Meredith quizzed.

Laura smiled. "I know how they did it. Remember when those papers fell out? They were all folded. Get it? They were folded small enough that someone could have slid them into Kim's locker through the vents in the door. They were all on top of her things, too, remember? When she opened the door, half of them fell out."

"She's right." Christine shook her finger at her friends. "Someone just stuffed Kim's locker full of yellow papers so we'd *think* she did it. And we fell for it—for a minute or two, anyway."

"That paper Scott found in his locker was folded, too," Nicki remembered. "And so was the one you found in your book bag, wasn't it, Meredith?"

Meredith nodded. "But all that means is that someone has to get the paper small enough to fit either in a locker or in my book bag. Anyone could have folded a paper."

"But who would want to?" asked Nicki. "And who would want to take Scott's dog?" She stirred her milk slowly. "Meredith, do you still have our list of suspects?"

Meredith nodded and pulled the list from her notebook. "Michelle Vander Hagen," read Nicki aloud. "Could she have planted the papers in Scott's and Kim's locker?" The other girls nodded. "Could she have taken Scott's dog?"

"She does live in the same neighborhood," said Christine. "But so does Corrin Burns. So do Nicki and I, for that matter."

"Me, too," said Meredith. "At least during the week."

Nicki looked back at the list. "Okay, let's try something else. Could Michelle have stolen Corrin's paper?"

"Practically anyone could steal anyone's paper anytime," Christine pointed out. "Just look at the benches out in the courtyard. There are at least fifty notebooks out there now, and there are probably ninety scattered all over the place in the morning before the warning bell rings."

"No one guards their notebook," shrugged Laura. "It's really silly to steal someone's homework, unless it's something like a math paper. It would be too easy to recognize the handwriting."

"That's *it*," squealed Meredith. "I know where we may find a *big* clue."

"Where?" asked Christine.

The bell rang. "You'll see next period in English," Meredith smiled.

Mr. Cardoza cleared his throat and put down his attendance roster. "Class, please take out your reading books and turn to page 67," he said, wiping his glasses.

Meredith raised her hand. "Mr. Cardoza, did you grade my research paper over the weekend?"

"Oh, yes," Mr. Cardoza leaned over his desk. "I have two papers to return to the owners." He peered over the top of his glasses. "I thought it was interesting that both papers were on Shakespeare."

Nicki bit her tongue to keep from squealing. So that's what Meredith meant! Corrin must have taken Meredith's paper and copied it!

Meredith had the same idea. "Mr. Cardoza," she asked, glancing at Corrin, "were the two papers a lot alike? Were they both on Shakespeare's *Hamlet*?"

"Actually, no," Mr. Cardoza's voice deepened. "Miss Burns' paper was on *Romeo and Juliet*. It was excellent and earned an *A*."

Meredith's jaw dropped as Mr. Cardoza handed a neatly typed report to Corrin, who smiled and cast a "ha ha" glance in Meredith's direction.

"Your paper, Miss Dixon, was not up to your usual fine standards," Mr. Cardoza frowned and looked at Meredith's quickly written report. "You had good thoughts here, but when I compared it to Miss Burns' paper, I felt I could not give it an *A*."

Meredith's paper had a *B+* written on the cover, and she looked slightly sick. "My first," she whispered to Nicki. "I've never made a *B* before.

"How could Corrin Burns write an *A* paper? Especially on Shakespeare?" Christine whispered.

"Maybe she just saw the movie," joked Laura.

"I'm sure she didn't read the play," Meredith grumbled. "It took me two solid weeks to read *Hamlet*."

"Maybe it's the curse," whispered Laura, her eyes wide.

"It's no curse," Nicki answered flatly. "Somebody's up to something and we've got to figure this out!"

"If we don't," Meredith said, looking sick, "I may never earn another *A* in my life!"

A student body meeting was held during sixth period. Mr. Padgett stood in the gym and waited for the movement in the bleachers to stop, and when everything was quiet, he picked up a microphone.

"As you know, we have a Fall Festival here at Pine Grove Middle School each October. As part of the festivities, we elect royal representatives from the student body. Seventh and eighth graders are eligible as long as they have a 3.5 grade point average. We will take nominations in homeroom next week."

Christine elbowed Nicki and nodded in Michelle Vander Hagen's direction. Michelle had bowed her head modestly when Mr. Padgett had mentioned the elections and now she was smiling as if it were a foregone conclusion she would win.

"What we need from you is an idea," Mr. Padgett went on. "Last year we had a harvest dance and the year before that we celebrated with a harvest hayride. I'm still getting hay out of my clothes from that one."

The teachers chuckled and the students rolled their eyes.

"If you have an idea or suggestion, pass it on to me or your homeroom teacher. Thank you for your attention, and have a good afternoon."

They were dismissed, and the girls stood up in the bleachers. "I have to go quickly," said Kim, pulling a stray piece of her dark hair behind her ear. "My mother is not well and I have to babysit for a neighbor. I will see you tomorrow."

Nicki watched her go. "I wish we could do something to help her," she said. "Kim isn't babysitting just to earn spending money, you know. I think Kim is trying to help her dad earn money for her mother's operation."

"What could we do?" Christine shrugged. "We're not made of money."

As if by instinct, every eye turned to look at Laura. "I'm not made of money either," she said nervously. "My mother is."

"Besides," Meredith shrugged, "I don't know if Kim's parents would take money if you just handed it to them. Some people are too proud to accept money from strangers."

"Could we help?" Nicki wondered.

"Don't know," Christine skipped down the bleachers. "Hey, you guys, can we stop in the locker room before we go home? I left my jacket in my gym locker."

The four girls walked through the darkened locker room and Laura shuddered. "This place is kind of spooky with the lights off."

"Nothing to worry about," smiled Christine. "I kind of like it like this." Looking at the girls, she moved to where her locker was and groped for the handle. "All you need is one week in a house with six kids and you'd like peace and quiet, too."

Her fingers found the handle and she opened the door. "Hey," she muttered, groping through the compartment. "My jacket's not in here. My gym clothes are, but what's this?" She pulled out a small bottle. The label read INDIA INK.

Nicki gasped. "That's not your locker, Christine. Yours isn't 48, it's 58. But whose locker is that?"

Meredith opened locker 58 one row over and pulled out Christine's denim jacket. Christine pulled a sweatshirt out of locker 48 and looked for a name. "I've found it," she muttered, holding the name tag up to the thin beam of light coming from the P.E. teacher's office. "You won't believe whose this is."

"Whose?" Laura asked.

"Michelle Vander Hagen's."

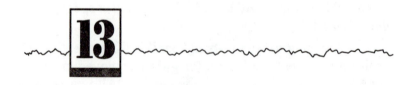

13

The next morning, Nicki, Laura, Christine and Meredith sat in chairs outside Mr. Padgett's office. "This is the first time I've ever been to the principal's office for something good," Christine said, fidgeting. "He'll be surprised to see me."

"Do you think we'll be heroes?" Laura asked.

"We ought to be," answered Nicki.

Mr. Padgett opened his door. "Come on in, girls," he said politely.

The girls filed in and sat on a couch against the wall in the principal's office. Mr. Padgett sat in a chair across from them. "Is this a social visit?" he asked casually. "Or can I help you girls with something?"

"We're here for two reasons," Nicki began. "First, we have an idea for the Fall Festival."

"I'm listening," the principal said.

"Why not have a Fall Festival Fair with games, a dunking booth, a cake walk and a craft sale?" Nicki asked. "There are a lot of people in town who would like to sell their crafts. But the most important part is that the admission charge and money from the school exhibits would be donated to a fund for Mrs. Park's kidney transplant."

"We know the Parks might not accept charity from strangers," Laura explained, "but this wouldn't be charity.

We'd earn it, and Kim could help us."

"You could crown the Fall Festival queen and king at the fair," Meredith added. "Every kid and parent in school would come out for that."

"The band could play . . . "

"The choir could sing . . . "

"And the shop students could make booths."

The girls laughed and Mr. Padgett smiled. "Girls," he said thoughtfully, reaching for his calendar, "I think that's a great idea. Can we pull it off in three weeks?"

"I think we can," Nicki nodded, "especially since we've found the person who has been painting lockers and causing trouble."

Mr. Padgett's eyebrows raised. "Who?"

"We found a bottle of India ink in Michelle Vander Hagen's locker," Meredith explained. "We didn't mean to snoop, but we know the same person who painted the lockers also drew that symbol on yellow papers with India ink."

"We think Michelle hid the ink in her gym locker because nobody ever checks through dirty gym clothes," Nicki said.

Mr. Padgett closed his eyes and thought a moment. "But why would Michelle do this?"

The girls looked at each other. "We're not exactly sure," Nicki hesitated, "but we think she is jealous of any girl who flirts with Scott Spence. That's why she painted Corrin's locker."

"But another locker was painted, too," Mr. Padgett pointed out.

"Yes," Nicki nodded slowly. "We think she painted

Scott's locker because a rumor got around school that Scott likes Kim Park. She was mad at Scott, too."

Mr. Padgett put his finger across his lips while he thought. Then he turned to Meredith. "Mr. Cardoza mentioned that you had a paper stolen, Meredith. Is that true?"

Meredith nodded.

"Why would Michelle steal a paper of yours? Were you flirting with Scott Spence, too?"

Meredith was quiet and looked at Nicki for help. "At first I thought Corrin Burns took my paper on Shakespeare and copied it," she said. "But then I found out Corrin did her paper on another play. I don't know why Michelle would take my paper, but I'm friendly with Kim and whoever is doing this is mad at Kim, too."

"Why?" Mr. Padgett asked.

"Jealousy," muttered Laura. "You don't know what a jealous woman will do!" She nodded wisely. "In *Jane Eyre*, a crazy woman ripped up Jane's wedding veil and burned down the house! There's no predicting the actions of a woman mad with jealousy!"

Mr. Padgett nodded and stood. "Thank you, girls," he said. "I'll call Michelle in later today and discuss these things with her. If I were you, I'd keep my suspicions to myself. Here at Pine Grove, someone is innocent until proven guilty, and frankly, that bottle of ink is only circumstantial evidence."

He patted Nicki on the back. "But your idea for a Fall Festival Fair is terrific. Let's go for it!"

"Christine, can your father announce the fair at the Christian school?" Nicki asked at lunch, remembering that

Mr. Kelshaw's school only enrolled first through fifth graders. "I'll bet the little kids would love our fair."

"Sure," Christine nodded. "We can have it announced at my church, too. Some of our people know the Parks. They have been visiting Kim's family."

Kim smiled. "My father likes the Christians. We are Buddhist, but the Christians have been kind to us."

"I can handle the publicity," Meredith offered. "My parents can have some posters printed up for us in the university printing office. It won't cost much at all."

"My parents know a lot of people in business," Nicki said. "I'll be in charge of signing up merchants to fill the booths."

Laura smiled. "I think I can talk my mother into loaning our car for the representatives to ride in. She'll probably want to make a donation, too."

"What can I do?" Kim wanted to know.

"You just take care of your mother and let your parents know we really want to help," Nicki smiled. "And talk your father into coming to the fair to pick up the money we raise for your mother's operation."

Michelle Vander Hagen walked up to the table. Her brown eyes were snapping with anger and her nose and eyes were red.

"Nicki Holland and company, I hate you!" she screamed.

Heads turned from every direction, and Nicki choked on her hamburger.

"How *dare* you accuse me to the principal! You were wrong! Who gave you the right to snoop around and accuse perfectly innocent people of stupid things like painting lockers! Who made you the great investigator?" Michelle stood there, her breaths coming in gulps, and Nicki saw that she was deadly serious and very, very angry.

"I'm sorry, Michelle, but we found those things accidentally," Nicki tried to explain.

"I don't care what you did, Nicki Holland," Michelle muttered, calmer now. She raised her chin and looked down on them. "That stupid bottle of ink wasn't mine. Someone must have stashed it in my locker. You were wrong, and you're a snoop, and I don't care who knows it."

Michelle spun on her heel and left. The girls simply looked at one another.

"I can't stand this," Laura muttered. "I feel just horrible. I think she's telling the truth."

"I don't feel too great myself," Nicki said, her food now tasteless. "I think we jumped to conclusions."

"We didn't have all the facts," Meredith mumbled. "And we knew better."

"I think we need to apologize," Christine said. "Although Michelle may never speak to us again."

"Half the school may never speak to us again," said Meredith, looking around. "Everyone heard Michelle. Everyone probably thinks we're either nosy or nuts."

"Including the real culprit," Nicki pointed out. "Somebody fooled us good."

"I don't care anymore," Laura said. "I'm afraid to go around looking for clues. What happens if we accuse the wrong person again?"

"We can't give up," Nicki was determined. "We'll just have to keep quiet until we're absolutely sure."

The next two weeks passed quickly. The girls worked hard on the Fall Festival, partly, Nicki realized, because they wanted to prove to their classmates that they weren't the traitors, snoops and awful human beings Michelle said they were. Laura worked especially hard, and Nicki noticed Laura was beginning to make friends everywhere.

Nicki tried to apologize to Michelle, but got only a stony glance in response. But on the Monday morning when the students voted for the seventh grade's Fall Festival king and queen, Michelle's iciness finally thawed.

"I forgive you, okay?" she told Nicki and her friends in homeroom. "I wouldn't want there to be any more hard feelings. Everyone knows now that I didn't do those weird things."

Mrs. Balian handed out the nomination forms. "Write in the name of the boy and girl you feel would be the best seventh-grade king and queen," she instructed. "After the votes are counted, the top five girls and guys will have their grade point averages evaluated by the teachers and the principal. The young man and woman with the highest grade point averages will be our Fall Festival king and queen."

Nicki looked at her nomination form. Who would make a good queen? She looked around the room. Michelle was beautiful, no doubt about it. She had not hesitated a minute and was busy writing in her choice for queen. *Herself, surely,* thought Nicki. But even though she was the most beautiful girl in school, she was so distant Nicki doubted if she had any good friends.

Corrin Burns could be a real pain if you weren't one of "her kind," but she was known around school as being a lot of fun. She had many friends, Nicki realized, although all of them were white, middle-class kids who dressed, walked and talked just like Corrin Burns.

Meredith was smart, probably the smartest kid to come through Pine Grove Middle School in twenty years, but most kids didn't relate to her very well. Christine was funny and mischievous, but too goofy to be royal. Kim was cute and smart, but she was still shy around people she didn't know. Aside from Nicki and her friends, Kim was a mystery to everyone else at Pine Grove.

Then there was Laura. Nicki looked at Laura, whose head was bent over her own nomination form. Laura was sweet, gentle, beautiful, rich, sophisticated and poised—plus she made good grades. In the last few weeks she had left the security of her best friends and made new friends at school, too. What better choice could there be? LAURA CUSHMAN, wrote Nicki on her form. Then she folded it and waited for Mrs. Balian to collect them.

In the seventh-grade class meeting that afternoon, Mr. Padgett didn't even have to wait to get everyone's attention. "I'd like to announce our Fall Festival representatives," he said, the microphone echoing in the unusual stillness. "But first, Mrs. Balian will make some announcements about this weekend's activities."

A groan rumbled through the bleachers, and Mrs.

Balian took the platform. "We want you to let your families know what will be going on next Friday and Saturday at the festival," she said. "The games, booths and kiddie rides will open at 4 P.M. on Friday and 10 A.M. on Saturday. Food vendors will serve hot dogs and hamburgers all day, so come prepared to eat!

"Band and choir members should be here at the school at six o'clock Friday evening for the mini-parade from the school to the fairground," she continued. "Our marching band will begin the parade, the choir float will follow and the car for our royalty will bring up the rear."

"So who won?" a voice called from the crowd.

Mrs. Balian frowned at the interruption and went on. "After the parade has arrived at the fairground, the seventh-grade king and queen will be crowned. Door prizes, which were graciously donated by area merchants, will then be awarded and presented by our queen. Make sure you and your parents are present. It's going to be a fun evening for everyone."

Mrs. Balian sat down. Mr. Padgett took the microphone. "Would you like to hear the names of our royalty?" he asked.

"YES!!" the crowd roared.

"The eighth grade representatives were announced earlier today in their class meeting," Mr. Padgett said. "Anne Taylor and Mark Todd. They will be crowned at the fair on Saturday night."

Mr. Padgett enjoyed the suspense. "First runner-up for king is Jeff Jordan," he finally said, his voice booming. "First runner-up for queen is Corrin Burns."

Nicki could see Corrin's friends buzzing. Twenty or thirty hands were slapping Jeff Jordan on the back. "If the seventh-grade representatives are unable to attend, these runner-ups will step in," explained Mr. Padgett.

"Are you ready?" Mr. Padgett called. Nicki could see Michelle Vander Hagen straighten up. Corrin Burns slumped; she looked defeated.

"Our Fall Festival king will be . . . Scott Spence!" The crowd roared, and Scott, who was sitting next to Jeff Jordan, grinned modestly.

"Our Fall Festival queen will be . . . Laura Cushman!" There was a gasp of surprise from the entire crowd, and Nicki couldn't help laughing. "Great! Laura, that's great!"

Laura's eyes were wide and her mouth open in a most un-Laura like expression. "Wh-what?" she stammered.

"You and Scott Spence!" squealed Christine, her face as red as her hair. "Can you imagine it?"

"Way to go, Laura," cheered Meredith. "You'll show them that brains and beauty *can* go together."

"This is good," smiled Kim. "You will make a good queen."

"That's it," called Mr. Padgett. "You're dismissed."

Everyone within five bleachers rose up to congratulate Laura, including Heather Linton and Julie Anderson. Nicki looked through the crowd for Michelle Vander Hagen, but she had disappeared. So, Nicki noticed, had Corrin Burns.

Instead of having her driver drop her off at Nicki's as she usually did, Laura asked him to pick all the girls up the next morning so they could ride to school in style. "I figured we could celebrate," she smiled, blushing.

"It's okay, your highness," said Christine, bowing her head. "We are your humble servants."

"Oh, cut it out," Laura was laughing.

"What will Michelle Vander Hagen do now?" Meredith asked. "I had the feeling she was living for the chance to be festival queen."

"She'll survive," Nicki said, gathering her books as the car pulled up alongside the school. "She'll tell us she's auditioning for Miss America or something."

Apparently Michelle had recovered. "Congratulations, Laura," she said, smiling as she came into homeroom. "But I think it is more important to be festival queen in the eighth grade, don't you?"

"Thank you," Laura answered politely, but she was puzzled.

"Don't let her get to you," whispered Nicki. "She's already planning her strategy for next year."

Scott Spence leaned over his desk. "Hey, Nicki! So there's royalty in your group now."

Nicki laughed and noticed Laura was rapidly becoming the color of her tomato-red sweater. "You'd better watch it, your majesty," Nicki called back. "If you abuse your position, the peasants may overthrow you."

"What we need, sire," Meredith bowed her head in Scott's direction, "is a little royal manpower. Can you get some of your servants and meet us at the fairground after school on Thursday? We've got to help put up booths and the platform."

"Consider it done," Scott replied, sending a salute in

Meredith's direction.

Scott and several of his friends did show up Thursday after school to help work on the fairground. The shop teacher and the art teacher had built frames for the booths, and now it was the students' job to assemble them. Everyone worked hard, and when it was all done, they were proud of their work.

Mr. Spence showed up at dinner time and brought soft drinks for everyone. "It looks great," Christine told Nicki as the girls rested on the large platform for the crowning of the king and queen. "Just think, it was all our idea. The fair will earn lots of money for Mrs. Park's operation, and everyone will have lots of fun, too."

"Best of all," Meredith said, "our good friend will be festival queen. When I think that Corrin almost won . . . "

"She didn't," Nicki cut her off. "So why spoil a beautiful afternoon thinking like that?"

They laughed and Nicki leaned back on her elbows to look over the fairground once again. Everything looked great, and Nicki knew the place would look even better when the merchants had filled the booths and people had filled the park. She looked once again at the banner that proudly proclaimed, "P.G.M.S. Presents the Fall Festival Fair." It fluttered gently in the afternoon breeze.

"What's that?" she sat up suddenly.

"What?" asked Meredith.

"That yellow thing hanging from the banner."

They all looked, and there it was—a yellow square hanging from the lower corner of the banner. "I'll go get it," volunteered Christine. She jumped from the platform and sprinted toward the banner.

She brought back a yellow paper folded twice. The

outside was marked "LAURA CUSHMAN."

"Look at those letters," Nicki said, pointing. "Remind anyone of anything?"

"Yes," Christine nodded. "It's the same style of writing on the paper in Scott's locker."

"The note that said DOG MEAT," Meredith added.

Nicki handed the paper to Laura. "I guess you should open it."

Laura's hand shook. "I don't want to hear anything about this curse stuff," she tried to laugh. Inside the yellow paper was the mystery mark, and underneath the twin figures were two words: STAY HOME.

15

Wow, Laura, you look pale," Christine said. "You're not scared, are you? You can't really believe in this curse stuff."

"Of course she doesn't," Nicki answered. But Laura's eyes were wide, and she nervously twisted her necklace.

"This is different," Laura said. "Meredith and Corrin lost their papers and Scott lost his dog, but what if someone tries something really serious tomorrow night?"

Christine put her arm through Laura's. "Relax," she said.

Nicki took the yellow paper and studied it. It was the same mystery mark drawn in the same ink. "Who could have done this?" Nicki wondered aloud.

"Who'd be mad at Laura for winning?" asked Christine. "Maybe we were wrong when we apologized to Michelle Vander Hagen. Maybe she's a really terrific actress and turned on the tears so we'd feel bad and leave her alone. She didn't want Laura to win! Michelle was all ready to be queen, but Laura snatched that crown right off her head."

"I didn't want to," Laura sighed weakly. "She can have it back."

"Oh, no," Meredith patted her on the back. "You're not going to give up. You're made of stronger stuff."

"Remember Scarlett O'Hara in *Gone With the Wind?*"

94

Nicki smiled. "She was from Georgia, just like you, and nothing scared her. You southern belles are tough!"

"Tough as nails," agreed Christine.

"Right now," Laura mumbled, "I feel more like Play Dough."

"Well, I wouldn't worry," added Meredith. "If Michelle couldn't win, she was going to make sure Laura didn't enjoy winning. She just wanted to scare you. She wouldn't *do* anything."

"I wouldn't be too sure," Laura sighed. "I think I would almost stay home, but my mother would kill me. She brought in an Atlanta designer to make my dress."

"You're kidding!" Christine shook her head in amazement. "I can't remember the last time I had a new dress. My clothes are all from my sister. I'm only grateful that Torrie has pretty good taste." She glanced down at her denim outfit. "This *is* okay, isn't it?"

"Sure it is," Nicki said. "But let's think about this note. How did that note get on the banner? Were any of our suspects around here today?"

"People have been here all day," said Christine. "The art class came before lunch and hung the banner. The shop classes came after lunch and dropped off the platform and the frames for the booths. There have been people in and out of here all day."

"Michelle is in the art class," added Meredith.

"And Heather, Julie and Corrin are in the choir. They brought their float out after lunch, too," Kim said.

"Okay, so anybody could have done it," Nicki sighed. "But this time I'm not going to make any accusations until we know *for sure* who the culprit is. There are still people around school who look at me strangely since that little episode with Michelle. If there's one thing I don't need, it's a reputation as a troublemaker."

"That's probably the last thing you'll ever have," Meredith smiled.

Laura lifted her head. "Okay, I'll go through with everything. I can be as tough as nails, too."

"Good!" Nicki said.

"Just promise me one thing?"

"What?"

Laura's shoulders dropped. "Please, please, will all of you ride in the limo with me and Scott? You can be the queen's ladies-in-waiting."

The girls looked at one another in delight.

Laura went on. "You're my best friends, and I need you there for support. I feel safer with all of you around."

Nicki could hardly sit still in class on Friday morning, she was so excited. "I don't think I'm going to be able to study today at all!" she whispered to Christine.

Christine grinned. "I know. Torrie helped me pick out a really nice dress to wear tonight and she's going to put a French braid in my hair."

"I don't know if you'll have time for that," said Laura. "I told Mrs. Balian ya'll were going to be my ladies-in-waiting and she suggested we have our pictures taken after school for the yearbook," she explained. "I'm having the limo driver bring my dress to school so I can change here. If you like, I can have him pick your dresses up, too."

"That'd be great!"

Laura turned to Kim. "Kim, honey, my mother wanted to get you something special in honor of your family. The driver is bringing a new dress for you, too."

Kim blushed and bowed her head. "*Kamsamnida* is the Korean word for thank you," she said. "Thank your kind mother for me."

"*Kam-sahm-nee-da*," Nicki whispered softly. Her first word in Korean.

Just then Mr. Padgett's voice interrupted the morning quiet. "Mrs. Balian, would you please send Nicki Holland to the office?" he asked.

"Certainly," she replied.

"And you may count both Michelle Vander Hagen and Corrin Burns present," Mr. Padgett went on. "They are here in the office."

"Fine," said Mrs. Balian. She looked at Nicki. "I suppose you'd better go now."

"Nicki, what's going on?" whispered Christine. "Do you think Mr. Padgett solved the mystery?"

"I don't know," Nicki whispered, gathering her books. "But I'll tell you all about it later. See you in science class."

When she heard the door of the office close, Mr. Padgett's secretary looked up and nodded briskly at Nicki. "Mr. Padgett's waiting in his office for you," she said.

Nicki knocked on his door. "Come in," the principal called.

In Mr. Padgett's office were Corrin Burns and Michelle Vander Hagen. Michelle glared at Nicki. *If looks could kill . . .* thought Nicki, and she took a seat facing Mr. Padgett.

"Nicki, I think we should talk," Mr. Padgett said.

"Good," Nicki answered. "There's something you should know, too, Mr. Padgett. Laura Cushman found one of those mystery mark notes yesterday, and it threatened her. She was almost afraid . . . " Nicki looked at Michelle, " . . . *almost* afraid to be crowned festival queen, but we talked her into it."

"Where did Laura find this note?" the principal asked.

"Actually, I found it," Nicki answered. "I saw it hanging from the banner at the fairgrounds."

"Very convenient," snapped Corrin Burns. "You saw the note and made *real* sure she saw it, didn't you?"

"What?"

"Nicki, these girls have brought proof to indicate that *you* are the guilty party in this little escapade," Mr. Padgett said sternly. "Corrin, let's see what you brought."

Corrin pulled several sheets of crumpled typing paper from her book bag. "This is Meredith Dixon's English paper," she said, practically snarling at Nicki. "I found it when I was helping Mr. Bracken clean up the science lab. It was in the cabinet next to your desk, Nicki Holland!"

"Did you take Meredith's report, Nicki?"

Nicki was horrified. "No, sir!"

"But she had the gall to say that I did!" Corrin fumed. "Meredith even asked Mr. Cardoza, in front of everybody, if my paper was a lot like hers. But it wasn't. And my paper got an *A*."

"Michelle, do you have something to say?" Mr. Padgett asked.

Michelle raised her chin. "At first I was just mad because Nicki and her friends accused *me* of doing these nasty things. But then I thought maybe *she* was the one who put that India ink stuff in my locker anyway. And as I thought more about it, I wondered who in the world would even know what that ink was, except the person who used it? *I'd* never heard of it. And then I realized that every time something has happened, Nicki Holland has been right there on the spot. It was all just a little too coincidental for me."

"Nicki, what would you like to say?"

Nicki was startled beyond words. She shook her head. "No," she said clearly. "I didn't do any of this. I'm trying to solve the mystery, not cause it."

"You're trying to *cause* it because you want to convince everyone you're Nancy Drew or something!" Corrin snapped.

"I think you're just trying to keep everyone's attention centered on yourself," Michelle said smoothly. "Well, it's not going to work for long."

"That's enough, girls," Mr. Padgett said. "I haven't exactly figured this out yet, but I do know that as long as there is a question, Nicki, I can't allow you to participate in the fair tonight. Since the festival was your idea, I was going to ask you to present the check to Mr. and Mrs. Park, but now that may not be appropriate."

He looked at the other two girls. "I don't know who is behind this," he said sternly, "but I have a hunch the problem lies with someone in this room. So I'll warn all three of you—stay away from Laura Cushman."

In less than an hour, the entire school had heard the

news. Nicki Holland was in some kind of trouble and even her best friends were avoiding her. Michelle Vander Hagen and Corrin Burns were saying that Nicki Holland was a thief, a snob and boy-crazy.

"Imagine," Michelle told a group of girls, "she was so crazy over Scott Spence that she stole his dog just so she could go over there and 'investigate'!"

The rumors were flying thick and fast. Kids who saw Nicki sitting at one table and her friends at another thought she was really Out. But they didn't know she was Out because she had asked to be.

"Come on, Nicki," Laura had begged. "We don't believe a word of that story."

"It isn't even logical," Meredith pointed out. "Even if your motive was genuine, you didn't have the opportunity to commit the crimes."

Christine glared at Meredith. "I don't care if you had motive *and* opportunity. I know you, Nicki, and I won't believe a word of it. You're our friend, and we believe in you. Come on and sit with us."

"No," Nicki shook her head stubbornly. "Mr. Padgett wants me to stay away from Laura, and I don't want him to think I'm going against him on purpose."

"I'll sit by myself," Laura offered.

Nicki shook her head again. "That's okay," she smiled. "That wouldn't be fair. I'll be fine. This will all be straightened out soon and things will be back to normal."

But Kim Park was loyal with a capital L. When Nicki put her tray down on an empty table, Kim followed and sat across from her.

"Kim, go back with the others," Nicki smiled. "It's

okay. Michelle and Corrin aren't going to get the best of me."

"No," Kim shook her head. "I am being a friend." With her hand she brushed the dark bangs out of her eyes. "Some people from Christine's church came to visit my mother," she said. "They read a beautiful poem about friendship."

Kim closed her eyes and recited in an older woman's voice: "Love is never glad about injustice, but rejoices whenever truth wins out. If you love someone, you will be loyal to him no matter what the cost. You will always believe in him, always expect the best of him, and always stand your ground in defending him."

Her eyelids fluttered open. "If that is not a poem about friendship, what is?"

Nicki smiled. "I think that's from the Bible."

"Then the Bible is a book about friends?" Kim asked.

"You could say that," Nicki answered. She noticed that Julie Anderson and Heather Linton were looking their way and whispering. "Look, Kim, the word is that I'm a stuck-up troublemaker. If you sit here, everyone will think you're stuck-up, too."

"That's okay," Kim smiled. Then she opened her mouth: "Get outta here, you little Chink." Corrin's voice.

Nicki's jaw dropped. "Corrin said that?"

Kim nodded. She opened her mouth again: "My father says you Japs are buying this country. I don't think we want you around here." Michelle's voice.

Nicki shook her head in amazement. "Michelle said that?"

Kim nodded. "I could do others," she smiled. "But I would prefer to sit here by my 'stuck-up' friend."

Nicki and Kim sat on a bench in the courtyard after school and watched Meredith, Christine and Laura head toward the girls' restroom to do their hair for the yearbook pictures. "You should go, too," Nicki told Kim. "Laura wants you to be part of her court."

"No," Kim said, still stubborn. In a voice not her own, she murmured: "If rain falls in the garden of my friend, I get wet."

Nicki grinned. "That's nice. Who said it?"

Kim bowed her head. "My mother."

Nicki leaned forward and rested her chin on her hands. "Right now the sun is shining on the garden of my friends, but I'm not exactly getting a sunburn.

"Let's think back to the scene of the first crime," Nicki said, closing her eyes. "Corrin Burns ran into class saying that her report had been stolen from her locker."

"The locker was open for about ten minutes," Kim added.

"Yes," Nicki nodded. "So apparently our culprit took the report during that time. But Corrin said she closed the locker and went to homeroom without noticing anything unusual. But when she came to English class . . . " Nicki paused and pushed her hands against her head, trying to remember. "When she came to English class she was carrying the yellow paper with the mystery figures on it."

"She said she found it in her locker," reminded Kim.

"So the culprit must have put the paper into her locker *after* she locked it again," Nicki muttered. "Just like the criminal filled your locker with papers and left a note for Scott."

"Little folded papers," smiled Kim, shaking her head. "I was new then. I didn't know what to think of them."

"You were being framed, that's all," Nicki sighed. "There was a paper in Scott's locker, a paper in Meredith's book bag, a yellow paper yesterday hanging from the banner . . . " Her eyes gazed off into the distance.

"I have those papers," she remembered, reaching for her notebook. She opened her notebook and pulled out the yellow papers. "Is there a clue in this collection?"

Kim looked at the four pages. "There is little difference in the mystery marks," she said. "All are done in India ink. Scott's paper says DOG MEAT . . . "

"Another attempt to frame *you*," said Nicki.

"And Laura's paper says STAY HOME."

"A direct warning to Laura."

"There is only one difference," Kim shrugged.

"What?" Nicki asked.

"This paper was not folded. It has no creases."

Nicki snapped her fingers. "That's the paper from Corrin's locker!"

Kim shook her head. "So?"

"Think, Kim. Do that trick of yours and remember exactly what Corrin told Mr. Cardoza on the day her paper was stolen."

Kim closed her eyes to think and in a moment she was speaking in Corrin's voice: "I stopped by my locker to pick up my research paper. I worked *so hard* on it, Mr. Cardoza. But I couldn't find it, so I took all my books out and then I found this!"

"What else did she say?" urged Nicki.

Kim wrinkled her forehead in concentration: "I left my locker open for about ten minutes this morning so Heather could pick up a book I borrowed. Someone must have taken my report then. I didn't notice anything until just now. My report is gone and *this* was on top of my books!"

"Don't you see? Corrin was lying! One minute she said the *unfolded* paper was the *last* thing she found, and the next minute she said it was on top of her books—as if someone had folded it and slipped it in through the vent." Nicki stood and clapped her hands. "So, unless someone knows Corrin's locker combination, there's no way this paper could have been in her locker unless *she* put it there herself."

"But we must know for sure," Kim reminded Nicki.

"Yes," Nicki grinned. "So let's find out."

Nicki walked over to the lockers and gingerly touched the mystery mark painted on Corrin's locker. It was ordinary spray paint, just like the paint on Scott's locker. These figures weren't as tiny or detailed as the ones on the yellow paper, but it was obvious what they were.

But what were they? Did they mean anything at all? Nicki looked at Kim. "Are you sure these aren't Korean?"

Kim nodded. "Some Chinese figures are similar to Korean letters, but these are not."

"Okay," Nicki tapped her fingers on the locker and thought.

"Hey," an angry voice cut through her thoughts. "What are you doing with Corrin's locker?"

It was Heather Linton with Julie Anderson by her side. *Oh, brother,* Nicki thought. *The Corrin Burns Fan Club.*

"I wasn't doing anything," Nicki said, shifting her books in her arms. "I just wanted to get another look at that paint job."

Julie snorted. "Going to paint another one, huh? Well, don't do my locker!"

"Why don't you find another cute guy and paint his?" Heather laughed. "That's why you do it, isn't it? So you can run over and bat your eyes and promise that *you'll* solve the crime."

"I've never painted anybody's locker," Nicki said. "I don't even know what that symbol means." She looked at the two girls. "Do you?"

"No way," laughed Heather. "Corrin says it looks like sixteenth notes."

Nicki smiled. "I didn't know Corrin was musical. She's not in the band, is she?"

Julie snorted. "Shows how much you know. Corrin has played the harp for years. Last year she even won an award for a harp composition."

"She's a composer? That's wonderful." Nicki turned to go, but she looked back at Heather. "By the way, Heather, I'd like to borrow the book you loaned to Corrin."

"What book?" Heather was puzzled.

"Remember? The day she left her locker open for you to pick up your book? The day her English paper was stolen."

Heather giggled. "Oh, yeah. You can't borrow that book."

"Why not?"

Julie snickered. "It's out of circulation."

Kim bowed slightly to the other girls. "Corrin Burns got an *A* on her English paper, yes? It must have been a magnificently good paper."

Julie and Heather looked at each other with tears of laughter in their eyes. "Of course it was good," Julie giggled. "She read the *Cliff Notes* instead of Shakespeare and changed the story into her own words. Her mother typed it."

"How intelligent," Nicki replied sarcastically.

"Yes," Heather missed the sarcasm in Nicki's voice. "Corrin Burns is smarter than you think."

Nicki looked at Kim. "I've got to do something now," she said, "and you need to go be with Laura and the others. It's a special day for you, and I don't want you to miss it."

Kim shook her head, but Nicki insisted. "If the sun shines on the garden of my friend, I feel warm," she smiled. "I'll be happy seeing you up there with the others. Come on, I'll walk you to Mrs. Balian's room."

Laura, Meredith, Christine and Mrs. Balian all greeted Nicki and Kim warmly. "We're meeting Scott and Mr. Padgett in the parking lot to take pictures around the limo and then Mr. Padgett's taking us out to dinner," Christine said. "Nicki, we sure wish you could come, too."

"That's okay," Nicki said, not wanting to admit how much she missed being with them. "I'm working on something."

"I really wish you were here," said Laura softly. "I'm still worried, Nicki. I'm not quite sure there isn't something to this curse business. I haven't felt good all day."

"That's just nerves," Mrs. Balian interrupted. "And we've got to get going if we're going to get you back here in time to change and ride over to the fairground for the crowning of our queen." Something in her smile made Nicki wonder if she really hadn't been a runner-up in the Miss America pageant.

"I've got to run, too," Nicki said, and before her friends could protest, she was out the door.

17

Nicki had never covered the mile between her home and school so quickly. Fortunately, her father was home and working at his big desk in the living room. Theirs was the only home she knew where the living room was a fully functioning office.

Mr. Holland was on the phone, but he raised a finger to let Nicki know he'd be off in a moment. "That will be fine, Mr. Jenkins," he smiled into the phone. "I'd be happy to meet with you next Thursday. Good-bye." He put the receiver down.

"What's up, Nicki-roo?" he asked. Nicki grinned. Her father came up with the strangest nicknames.

"I need a favor, Dad. Actually," she sat on the edge of his desk, "it's a favor for a friend. She's afraid she's been cursed and she's really worried about being crowned queen at the Fall Festival."

"Laura Cushman?" her dad asked. "The girl who lost her father last year?" Nicki kept her parents pretty well-informed about her friends.

"Yes. Anyway, Laura got a threatening note and she's scared someone's going to try to do something tonight. I was supposed to stick around and help her, but there's somewhere else I have to be." Nicki hugged her knees. "Could you stand in the crowd near Laura and make sure no one throws a pie in her face or anything like that?"

Mr. Holland smiled. "When you flash that dimple, young lady, you know I can't say no. I'll have Joshua and Sarah with me, though. Mom is supposed to join us after she shows a house at six-thirty, but I'll probably have my hands full."

"That's okay, Dad." Nicki knew how active her little brother and sister could be. "Just stand in the front of the crowd and keep an eye out—you know, like a Secret Service man. They're supposed to crown the king and queen at seven o'clock."

Mr. Holland nodded. "I'll defend her from enemies, foreign and domestic, at peril of my life and limb. I promise."

Nicki rolled her eyes. "Just please don't let anyone trip her or throw mud in her face."

The school was still quiet when Nicki slipped through the large double doors at five-thirty. She padded down the wide halls toward Mrs. Balian's room, wincing once when her sneakers made a loud squeak across the tile floor.

If she had timed it right, Laura and the girls would be halfway through supper now. Soon they'd be coming back here to change clothes and drive to the fairground. While Mr. Holland guarded Laura from mischief at the fairground, Nicki had a job to do at school.

What would the culprit do to Laura Cushman? Was that note intended only to scare her? Nicki had thought about it all afternoon. So far, the culprit had stolen three times—two reports and a dog, even though the dog was returned a day later. *I guess McArthur was too much even for our mystery culprit to handle,* Nicki thought. *I wonder how she explained that to her parents. Dog-sitting?*

Nicki didn't think the culprit would physically hurt Laura—there would be too many people around to do that. Stealing and vandalism seemed to be more her style.

The door to Mrs. Balian's room was unlocked, so Nicki slipped in and felt her way through the darkness of the windowless room. The window in the door had been papered over to give the girls privacy while dressing, allowing only a tiny bit of light to filter into the room.

Nicki walked to the tall closet on the side of the room and stepped in. She closed the door halfway and settled down into a comfortable position. *Not bad,* she thought. *Now we'll wait and see what happens.*

As her eyes adjusted to the dark, she was able to see a row of dresses hanging against the opposite wall. Knowing her friends as she did, she could tell immediately which dress went with which girl.

Torrie Kelshaw's dark green taffeta dress was first in the line, obviously intended tonight for Christine. A black knit dress with a bright red vest looked as long and lean as Meredith, and a simple but elegant white dress with a black bow was apparently the dress Mrs. Cushman had bought for Kim. *She'll love it,* thought Nicki. *That black bow will look adorable with her black hair.*

Apart from the others was the most breathtaking dress Nicki had ever seen. It was a deep aqua taffeta, the identical color of Laura's eyes, and studded with beads and rhinestones on the bodice. A full, short skirt completed the outfit, and nearby Nicki could see a shoebox with what looked like aqua heels. Laura really would look like a queen.

A feeling of self-pity swept over Nicki. *I could be with them instead of hiding in a closet if only . . .* If only what? If only someone weren't out to get them all in trouble? If only she had been able to solve the mystery sooner?

No sense in moping now, Nicki told herself sternly.

The door to Mrs. Balian's room clicked, and Nicki drew her breath in suddenly. Something fluttered in her stomach, and she automatically reached out to draw the closet door a few more inches toward her.

Someone slipped into the room, and whoever it was, it wasn't Mrs. Balian and a group of noisy girls. A dark figure moved quietly through rows of desks and stood in front of the dresses, waiting.

She can't see, Nicki realized. *It's too dark and her eyes haven't adjusted yet!*

Nicki pushed the closet door open wider. The figure didn't move. It was a girl, dressed in black, and she was holding something in her right hand.

Nicki slipped out of the closet as the girl in black moved toward Laura's dress. Her hands came together as Nicki called, "STOP!"

The girl jumped, then threw whatever she was holding over her head. Nicki moved toward the door and flicked on the light switch.

There stood Corrin Burns, dressed in a beautiful black skirt and black silk blouse. Nicki looked around the room and found the object Corrin had thrown. "A bottle of India ink!" Nicki cried, reaching for the bottle. "You were going to pour this over Laura's dress!"

Corrin didn't answer, and as Nicki picked up the bottle, she realized Corrin had loosened the cap. Ink was now running over Nicki's fingers.

"Gross," Nicki sighed. "This stuff is murder to clean." She looked up at Corrin. "I know you did everything, Corrin.

You didn't have your paper ready when it was due, so you just made up that story about a curse and the mystery mark. You enjoyed the attention so much you kept the story up for a while, didn't you?"

"Oh, yeah?" Corrin flung her brown hair out of her eyes. "You're the one with ink all over your hands, Nicki Holland. I can just say that I found *you* here about to ruin your friends' dresses. You just couldn't handle being left out!"

The door clicked again, and this time Mrs. Balian entered, followed by Laura, Kim, Meredith and Christine. "Look!" Corrin shouted, pointing to Nicki. "I came in to wish you all good luck, and I found Nicki here with India ink. She was going to ruin everything for you all! Look at her hands!"

Laura's eyes were wide. "Nicki Holland," she whispered. "I can't believe it!"

18

Nicki looked at Laura. "Laura, you don't honestly believe that story, do you?"

Laura shook her head. "I'm so upset. I don't know what to believe."

Mrs. Balian reached for a paper towel in her desk drawer. "I'm glad I have these," she smiled. "You never know when an emergency is going to come up." She took the leaking bottle of ink and tossed it into the garbage can. "Now, girls, someone had better do some explaining."

Corrin began to sputter. "I came in here to congratulate Laura. I'm first runner-up, after all, and I thought I should come and say something, just to show there were no hard feelings. But when I turned on the light, there stood Nicki Holland with that bottle of ink. She was ready to throw it on those dresses!"

Mrs. Balian raised an eyebrow. "Then why were you near the dresses and Nicki nearer the door? It seems like you two should have been in opposite positions."

Corrin nodded. "I wasn't finished. When I saw what she was about to do I ran over here to stand in front of the dresses. Then Nicki got scared, I guess, and started to run out the door, but you came in."

"I see." Mrs. Balian motioned for Meredith, Christine, Laura and Kim to sit down. "Laura, do you believe that Corrin was coming here to congratulate you?"

There was fire in Meredith's eyes. "The Atlantic Ocean would freeze over first," she sputtered.

"I was talking to Laura, Meredith," Mrs. Balian said.

Laura shook her head. "I'd like to hear Nicki's story, Mrs. Balian. She's been my friend for months, and she's never lied to me."

Mrs. Balian turned to Nicki. "What's your story?"

"It all began the day Corrin didn't have her English research paper done, Mrs. Balian. She told Mr. Cardoza that someone had stolen it from her locker."

"How could someone steal a report from a locker?" Mrs. Balian asked.

"She had Heather Linton and Julie Anderson say that Corrin had left her locker open for ten minutes. They knew she just hadn't done the report. But they didn't know that later she planted the yellow paper with the mystery mark. She just did that because she didn't like Kim Park."

"Lots of people found those yellow papers," Corrin muttered, sitting down. "What makes you think I put that paper in my own locker?"

"Because you wanted attention," Nicki said, walking to the closet where she had left her bookbag. "You thought being 'cursed' would make someone like Scott Spence notice you more."

"Oh, we all noticed you," Meredith chuckled. "The way you carried on was too much!"

Nicki pulled out her notebook. "Here are the four papers. This one that says DOG MEAT was found in Scott's locker. You were still trying to frame Kim, and you heard that Scott thought Kim was cute." Nicki shrugged, "Kim is cute, but why should that bother you? Are you *afraid* of someone a little different?"

Corrin didn't answer so Nicki went on. "You ruined Scott's report and tried to convince him that Kim did it so he'd stay away from her."

"That's nuts," Corrin glared at Nicki.

"No, it makes sense," Kim answered. "Nicki mentioned in her geography report that dogs are sometimes used for food in Korea. It was that afternoon Scott's locker was painted and he found his note. At the same time, I heard someone in the girls' water closet—excuse me, restroom— whisper something about having paint on her fingers. We knew that whoever painted the lockers with the mystery mark had to be a girl."

Nicki picked up the story. "Scott's dog, McArthur, was taken on Saturday, but came home on Sunday morning. Corrin lives in Scott's neighborhood and could easily have opened the gate and led him to her house that morning. Scott said the dog was so friendly, he'd go with anyone. But he eats so much that Corrin couldn't afford to keep him long. She just turned him out of her yard on Sunday, but not before she put a yellow kerchief around his neck to keep the story of the 'curse' alive. McArthur went straight home."

"Now it seems so simple," Christine said. "But what about Meredith's curse?"

"This page," Nicki said, pulling another yellow paper from her notebook, "was the paper Meredith found in her bookbag when you stole her research paper on Shakespeare."

"Now why would I do that?" Corrin demanded to know. "I handed in my own paper on Shakespeare, and I got an *A* on it. I didn't copy Meredith's paper!"

"Of course not," Nicki smiled. "That would be too obvious, since no one in this school talks or even *thinks* quite like Meredith. But you desperately needed an *A*, and you knew you couldn't get one by yourself. So you got your information from *Cliff Notes* and to make sure your paper wouldn't look bad next to Meredith's, you took hers and left this yellow paper so everyone would think the mysterious curse was alive and well."

"I did manage to turn in a paper," Meredith explained to Mrs. Balian, "but I had to write it from memory, and it wasn't typed. I got the first *B* of my life on it."

"Why would Corrin Burns suddenly care so much about her grades?" Christine asked. "I've known her since sixth grade, and Corrin's never cared about her grades before."

"No," Meredith said, snapping her fingers as the realization hit her, "but being queen of the Fall Festival was never open to Corrin before. And from the five most popular girls in school, the queen is the one who has the highest grade point average. Corrin probably wouldn't even had made first runner-up without that *A* in English."

"That makes sense," said Christine, nodding in Corrin's direction.

"When you found out that I told Mr. Padgett we suspected Michelle Vander Hagen, you teamed up with her to frame *me*, didn't you?" asked Nicki. "You unearthed Meredith's report as evidence against me. What Michelle didn't know, though, is that you're the one who stashed the ink in her locker."

Corrin turned her face away.

"This page," Nicki pulled out the page marked for Laura, "was a simple warning for Laura not to come to the fair tonight. If Laura had not come, Corrin would have been crowned queen because she was first runner-up."

"She'd be standing up there next to Scott Spence," Christine murmured. "No wonder she was willing to go so far."

"Now I understand," Laura said, her aqua eyes wide. "When I decided to go through with the ceremony tonight, Corrin showed up here to ruin my dress. She knew I'd never go up on that platform in a ruined dress, and there wouldn't be time to bring another dress from home."

"Look at Corrin," Meredith said, pointing to her outfit. "She's dressed to play the part of a queen."

Corrin blushed. "Of course I dressed up for tonight. As first runner-up, I thought maybe I'd have to do something in front of everybody. Plus, I'm singing in the choir."

"No," Nicki shook her head. "You and I weren't even supposed to go to the fair tonight. Mr. Padgett told us to stay away from Laura Cushman."

"Then what are you doing here?" Corrin glared at Nicki and stood up. "You haven't proven anything, Nicki Holland, and I'm leaving."

"Wait just a moment, Corrin," Mrs. Balian said. "I don't believe Nicki is finished." Corrin sank back into her chair.

"No, I'm not finished." Nicki held up the remaining sheet of yellow paper. "This paper has been through a lot. Corrin found it in her locker when her report was stolen, right Corrin?"

Corrin was pouting, but she nodded.

"I splashed it with water once to make sure this black writing was done in India ink, and it's been riding around in my notebook for weeks. But if you look closely, you can see that this page has never been folded."

Nicki handed the page to Mrs. Balian. "Corrin had to put this paper into her locker herself because anyone else would have had to fold it to slip it through the locker vent. Corrin couldn't say the paper was left in her locker when her report was stolen, because Heather had said she hadn't seen the yellow paper when she supposedly went to Corrin's locker. I guess Corrin didn't fill Heather in on her entire plan."

"I feel so stupid," Meredith muttered. "That clue was in front of us the whole time."

"Heather and Julie knew Corrin hadn't done her paper, but they didn't know Corrin was planning to invent the mystery mark and blame everything on Kim Park," Nicki said. "She couldn't even trust her best friends with that secret."

Corrin put her head down on her desk. "Corrin also knows about India ink because she's a musician," Nicki said. "She even won an award for a harp composition."

"Why, Corrin," Mrs. Balian smiled. "I didn't know you were so talented."

Corrin lifted her head and Nicki was surprised to see that her eyes were filled with tears. "No one plays a stupid harp," she muttered. "I didn't want anyone to know. It's not cool to come to school with a harp on your back, for pete's sake."

"Corrin, you don't have to worry about what people will think of you," Mrs. Balian said gently. "It takes all kinds of people to live in the world. We should appreciate our differences. I think it's lovely you can play the harp."

Corrin folded her arms and Nicki could see that her chin was quivering. Kim stood up and placed her hand on Corrin's shoulder. "I do not hate you," she said, smiling, "just because you play the harp."

"That's about it," Nicki told Mrs. Balian. "There's only one thing that we haven't been able to figure out."

Kim smiled. "The meaning of the painted letters," she said. "The writing is not Korean."

Corrin shrugged and wiped a tear from her cheek. "I don't know what it means, either. I saw it on some frozen Chinese vegetables my mother was cooking. It was easy to remember because it looked like sixteenth notes."

"Chinese!" Kim beamed. "I thought so."

"Corrin, this will have to be settled later, but I think Nicki has done a convincing job of tying up loose ends," Mrs. Balian smiled. "I think you'll have some apologies to give, some lockers to repaint, and Mr. Cardoza will have to adjust those grades on that English paper."

"I still have your report," Corrin mumbled to Meredith. "It's a little wrinkled, but it's readable. You can give it to Mr. Cardoza."

Meredith sighed in relief. "Good. I won't have a *B* on my record anymore."

Christine giggled. "I wish I had a *B*. I only got a *C* on my cockatiel paper."

"We're running out of time," Mrs. Balian checked her watch. "Corrin, you'll find Mr. Padgett waiting outside with the limo driver. I want you to go and tell him the truth of what happened. Laura, you and the girls have got to get dressed now or we'll be late." She winked at Laura. "We don't want to keep the king waiting, do we?"

They all laughed and Meredith, Christine and Kim stood to get dressed. Laura sat down by Nicki. "I don't know what to say," she said, her eyes down. "For a minute there, I didn't know what was going on. I was confused, and I'm sorry

I doubted you if even for a minute."

"It's okay, Laura," Nicki said. "Things did get confusing for a while. But I'm your friend, and you can trust me." She laughed and mimicked Laura's southern drawl. "Ah promise."

19

Standing with her family in the crowd, Nicki watched as Laura Cushman was crowned seventh-grade queen of the Pine Grove Middle School Fall Festival. Kim, Christine and Meredith stood behind her, smiling, and Scott Spence stood next to Laura and tried to act cool. But when he caught Nicki's eye, he grinned and winked. Wow.

Mr. Holland saw the wink, too. "Who *is* that young man?" he asked, teasing. "Is he the one who might throw a pie in Laura Cushman's face?"

Nicki punched her father playfully. "He's just a friend, Dad. And you don't have to worry about Laura anymore."

Mrs. Holland glanced over at her daughter. "Honey, why aren't you up there with all your friends?"

"It's a long story, Mom," Nicki answered. "I'll tell you later."

Mr. Padgett called Mr. and Mrs. Sang Soo Park to the platform and introduced them to the crowd. "Our newest student comes from the farthest away," he said, pulling a reluctant Kim to the front of the platform. "But Kim has made remarkable progress learning our language and making new friends."

Mr. Padgett smiled at Kim. "Is there anything you would like to say?"

Kim blushed, but stepped toward the microphone. "I would like to thank the students and teachers of Pine Grove Middle School for this night," she said. "But most of all I would like to thank Nicki Holland, who wanted to help my family. She also wanted to be my friend."

Mr. Padgett searched the crowd. "Nicki, would you come up here?"

Nicki felt a bit uncomfortable in her blue jeans since everyone else was dressed up, but she climbed the platform steps and stood next to Kim.

"As the principal of the school, I've learned to solve problems one at a time," Mr. Padgett told the crowd, "but Nicki Holland and her friends have solved more than one problem today. Nicki, would you like to give this check to Mr. and Mrs. Park?"

Nicki took the check Mr. Padgett handed her. "Mr. and Mrs. Park, we'd like to give you this check for . . . " Nicki couldn't believe it! "Ten thousand dollars! Wow!" She grinned. "It's to cover the expenses for your wife's operation," she explained as she handed it to Mr. Park. Mr. Park bowed, and Nicki and Mr. Padgett clumsily bowed in return. Then Mr. Park turned and bowed to Laura, Scott and the girls, and they bowed back. When Mr. Park bowed toward the audience, Nicki saw her dad trying to bow, too.

Nicki skipped down the steps and took her father's arm. "That's enough, Dad," she said, laughing. "Later I'll introduce you and you can shake his hand."

But when the ceremony was finished, Nicki was surrounded by her friends, including Scott and Jeff Jordan.

"I wish you had been with us," Laura said. "It just wasn't the same without you."

"That's okay," smiled Nicki, remembering Scott's

wink. "Being in the audience wasn't bad. You all looked great!"

"Let's go *do* something," urged Christine, shifting in her shoes. "My heels are killing me and I'm hungry."

"Didn't you just come from dinner?" Nicki couldn't believe Christine's appetite.

"She was too nervous to eat," Meredith explained. "They served spaghetti and Christine didn't want to slurp it in front of Mr. Padgett."

"How about an egg roll?" Nicki suggested, spotting a Chinese food vendor among the booths. "I didn't get any supper and I'm starving."

The group placed their orders and were waiting patiently when Scott elbowed Nicki. "Look," he smiled. "On that sign over there. It's the mystery mark!"

The girls leaned forward for a better look and the cook walked up. "May I help you?" he asked politely. "I am Larry Cho, the owner."

"Mr. Cho," Christine pointed, "what does that sign mean?"

"In particular, what is the meaning of the third symbol?" added Meredith.

Mr. Cho nodded. "Roughly translated, the sign says, 'Better is a meal with friends than a meal with kings.' That third symbol there is *peng*. It is the Chinese word for friendship."

"That's amazing," Laura smiled, turning toward her friends. "All along, Corrin's curse meant nothing but friendship."

Nicki grinned and raised her cup. "Even though there *is* royalty among us, here's to a meal with true friends—

whether or not they are kings and queens."

*   *   *   *

Don't miss the next exciting adventure of Nicki, Meredith, Christine, Laura and Kim . . .

The Case of the Phantom Friend

A man's angry voice echoed in the house and reached the girls outside. "You're a foolish, silly old woman!" the man yelled. "And one of these days you'll realize how wrong you are to oppose me. Just you wait, old lady. You'll be sorry!"

Nicki, Laura, Christine, Meredith and Kim have found a new friend in Lela Greaves. But someone has threatened Mrs. Greaves and now she could lose everything she loves. The girls have one clue that they hope will lead to something to save Mrs. Greaves—if only they can solve the mystery before it's too late!

About the Author

Angie Hunt lives in Largo, Florida, with her husband Gary, their two children, and a Chinese Pug named Ike. Her favorite color is periwinkle blue, she makes quilts and she takes Tae Kwon Do with a group of middle schoolers. She and Gary have been serving in youth ministry for fourteen years, and she writes a monthly column called "Ask Angie Anything" for her church kids. She weighed 86 pounds in the eighth grade . . . but she doesn't tell her weight anymore.

Don't Miss Any of
Nicki Holland's Mysteries!